CANYON ECHOES

CANYON ECHOES 8

TYNDALE KiDS

TYNDALE HOUSE PUBLISHERS, INC., CAROL STREAM, ILLINOIS

RED ROCK MYSTERIES

#1 BEST-SELLING AUTHORS

JERRY B. JENKINS · CHRIS FABRY

Visit Tyndale's website for kids at www.tyndale.com/kids.

TYNDALE is a registered trademark of Tyndale House Publishers, Inc.

Tyndale Kids logo is a trademark of Tyndale House Publishers, Inc.

Canyon Echoes

Copyright © 2005 by Jerry B. Jenkins. All rights reserved.

Cover and interior photographs copyright © 2004 by Brian MacDonald. All rights reserved.

Authors' photograph © 2004 by Brian MacDonald. All rights reserved.

Designed by Jacqueline L. Nuñez

Edited by Lorie Popp

Published in association with the literary agency of Alive Communications, Inc., 7680 Goddard Street, Suite 200, Colorado Springs, CO 80920.

This novel is a work of fiction. Names, characters, places, and incidents either are the product of the authors' imaginations or are used fictitiously. Any resemblance to actual events, locales, organizations, or persons, living or dead, is entirely coincidental and beyond the intent of either the authors or publisher.

For manufacturing information regarding this product, please call 1-800-323-9400.

Library of Congress Cataloging-in-Publication Data

Jenkins, Jerry B.
  Canyon echoes / Jerry B. Jenkins, Chris Fabry.
    p. cm. — (Tyndale kids) (Red Rock mysteries ; 8)
  Summary: While on vacation at Lake Powell and the Grand Canyon, thirteen-year-old twins Bryce and Ashley try to prevent the theft of a famous tennis player's necklace, only to land their entire family in danger.
  ISBN 978-1-4143-0147-1 (pbk.)
  [1. Robbers and outlaws—Fiction. 2. Necklaces—Fiction. 3. Twins—Fiction. 4. Powell, Lake (Utah and Ariz.)—Fiction. 5. Grand Canyon National Park (Ariz.)—Fiction. 6. Christian life—Fiction. 7. Mystery and detective stories.] I. Fabry, Chris, date. II. Title. III. Series
  PZ7.J4138Can 2005
  [Fic]—dc22   2005011955

Printed in the United States of America

17   16   15   14   13   12   11
9   8   7   6   5   4   3

This book is thankfully dedicated to three families:
Deborah, Michael, Elise, and Ian Hoskins
Tom, Peggy, and Corinne Turney
Libby, Thomas, Devon, and Adrienne Theune

"LOTS OF PEOPLE
have DIED THERE, you know."
Marion Quidley

"A VACATION is
having nothing to do and
all day to do it in."
Robert Orben

"A VACATION is
what you TAKE when you
can no longer take
what you've been taking."
Earl Wilson

PART 1

CHAPTER 1

◔ *Bryce* ◔

I gunned my **ATV,** and air whooshed through my helmet. My twin, Ashley, kicked up dust ahead of me, so I swerved outside her path. We neared the red rock formation our town is named after, and Ashley veered in front of me.

"Gaining on you," I said into my headset microphone.

"Eat my dust," she said, laughing.

The sun beat down like a police interrogation light. Good thing we were slathered in sunscreen. Lots of skin cancer in Colorado. Can't be too careful.

I suggested the race after waiting all day for a vacation update.

Our stepdad, Sam, had thrown out several hints and offered all the money in the change jar to anyone who guessed our destination. Mom made us stay away from the mailbox, so I figured she was waiting for airline tickets or brochures from some resort. I even checked caller ID, but Mom deleted a couple of calls.

I pulled up beside Ashley, but she made one last push to the finish line and raised a fist. She slid to a stop beside a boulder near a hiking trail. "Beat you! I beat you!"

"Two out of three," I said.

"No way! Just admit I owned you."

"I let you win."

She did a little victory dance on her ATV. When we first started riding, Ashley wouldn't go faster than 10 miles an hour. Now, as long as she knew the road, she'd go as fast as me. Well, faster in this case.

We sat there going over Sam's clues again. He had said where we were going was "one of seven," "about 500," and "two."

"Doesn't make sense," Ashley said. "Could it be one of the seven highest mountains in Colorado?"

My cell phone rang. It was Mom.

"Sam and I are ready," she said. "Time to find out where we're going."

Ashley fired up her ATV. "Last one home has to sit next to Dylan!"

CHAPTER 2

❀ Ashley ❀

Sitting beside our little brother isn't such a bad thing really. He's almost five and very cute, and he says funny things. On long car trips he falls asleep, and the bouncing makes drool drip from his lips. Leigh, our stepsister—she's going to be a senior at Red Rock High— seems to like him more than the rest of us combined. She plays with Dylan and takes him on walks, probably because he almost died on one of our adventures.

Pippin and Frodo barked at us as we zoomed up to the back door. I beat Bryce but as I was setting my brake and turning off the machine, he jumped off and blasted through the back door before me.

We argued about who had won all the way through the kitchen and found Sam, Mom, Leigh, and Dylan in the living room.

You get a feeling just before vacation that's like no other. The packing, the excitement of going to a new place, leaving your chores, getting carsick. Red Rock is nice and it feels more and more like home (we moved from Illinois), but it's good to get away. Makes it fun to come back to your own room.

"There's $45 in the pot," Sam said. He's tall and muscular with hair that's turning gray, a mustache that covers his whole upper lip, and a voice as low as a tuba. Bryce and I used to call him The Cowboy. Mom wasn't a Christian when they got married, but now she is. Bryce and I are too, but Sam and Leigh aren't there yet. Maybe because of what happened to Sam's wife and little daughter. They died in the same plane crash our real dad died in. Sam was working for the government at that time, and terrorists thought he was on the plane, so they shot it down. He and Mom met at one of the memorial services.

Mom had a basket with strips of paper inside. "First guess is Dylan's." She unfolded his strip, and I saw Leigh's handwriting. "It says, 'Thomas the Tank Engine.'"

We all laughed. Then Mom read Leigh's guess. "'Santa Fe, New Mexico.' Good guess."

Leigh raised her eyebrows. She wasn't going with us because she was house-sitting for one of Mom's friends, plus watching Pippin and Frodo.

Mom opened the next guess. "'Cancun.'"

I gave Bryce a look.

"I can dream, can't I?" he said.

Mom unfolded the last piece of paper. "'Breckenridge.'" She smiled. "Sounds nice this time of year."

Sam sucked in a big breath. "All good guesses. Great ideas for next year. But all wrong. The money is safe."

"I'm starting a new book," Mom said. "The main characters take a trip west. . . ."

Sam said, "And instead of me flying us somewhere—"

"Would you guys stop?" Bryce said. "This is killing us!"

Sam smiled. "Okay. I said 'two' because we're not going to one place, but two."

"And 500?" Bryce said.

"It's about 500 miles away. A little farther to the second place."

"And seven?" I said.

"It's one of the world's seven natural wonders. West of us."

"The Grand Canyon!" Bryce and I said together.

I'd never been west of Colorado, but I'd heard a lot about the Grand Canyon. It didn't seem as fun as a resort, but I tried not to look disappointed.

"What's the second place?" Bryce said.

Sam stuck a DVD in the player. "Lake Powell, north of the canyon. We're renting a houseboat."

"No fair!" Leigh said.

"You can still come," Mom said. "We can find somebody else to do your jobs."

"Yeah, I bet they'd even let Randy come," Bryce said.

Leigh frowned at Sam, and something passed between them. She moved to the stairs. "No. I'll stay here and earn money for my car. But I wish you'd told me where you were going."

CHAPTER 3

☺ *Bryce* ☺

I tried not to let it show, but I wasn't that excited about the Grand Canyon and a boat on some lake. Sam must have noticed, because once the DVD started, my mouth dropped open and I couldn't shut it.

The DVD began with a bald eagle spreading its wings and floating over blue water that looked like an ocean. The camera panned over huge rock formations rising from the water.

The lake was formed in 1963 when they built the Glen Canyon Dam on the Colorado River. The lake is 186 miles long—that's not a misprint—186 MILES. The coastline is longer than the distance from Seattle to San Diego.

This was more than a pond. This was a lake on some kind of water-enhancing drug.

Still, I wished we were going to a deserted island where we could run along the beach. That was before the DVD showed beaches and kids riding water skis. And Sea-Doos, those things that look like ATVs for water. Then a man and his son holding up fish—walleye and largemouth bass.

"I'm in," I said.

The announcer on the DVD sounded like the guy who talks over the movie trailers at the theater. His voice was deeper than the Grand Canyon. ". . . And you'll enjoy this spectacular scenery and relaxed surroundings in the comfort of your very own hotel on the water."

A houseboat half the size of Texas drifted by. The people on it must have been the children of orthodontists, because their teeth were straight and as white as polar bears in a blizzard. I couldn't take my eyes off the screen. The boat had a huge theater, four luxury rooms, a gourmet kitchen (Mom groaned and said she wouldn't be cooking), a gas grill, a huge slide off the back, and more.

"When do we leave?" I said.

Mom shushed me.

The next shot was from a helicopter and made my stomach lurch. It flew south, past a dam, and the deep-voiced announcer said, "And you're only a short distance from one of the most breathtaking vacation destinations in the world: the Grand Canyon."

"What are we going to do there?" Ashley said.

"A four-day hike," Mom said. "It'll be the experience of a lifetime."

CHAPTER 4

❀ Ashley ❀

There was a lot to look forward to, but I have a habit of seeing the glass half empty. Show me the perfect resort and I'll find the only broken vending machine.

The lake looked like it could be fun, but it would be better if there were kids there we knew. I figured Mom would make Bryce and me watch Dylan every day.

What worried me most was that there wouldn't likely be any mystery Bryce and I could solve. We'd been on a roll.

The next day after dinner I drove to Marion Quidley's. She had presented a report on the Grand Canyon the year before. Marion enjoys lights in the desert, UFOs, Bigfoot, and conspiracy theories.

She once told me that she thought our speech teacher was communicating with space aliens.

I couldn't figure out why Marion was weird, but then I discovered her father had been hurt in an accident and was bedridden at home. Maybe that was why she distracted herself by reading—and believing—strange things and getting into life on other planets. Her own life wasn't working out that well, so maybe this gave her something else to think about.

We took a walk behind her house. She said her dad wasn't doing well, that he had caught a virus from some visiting relatives.

She handed me a white box. "It's my lucky compass," Marion said. "Mom and I were driving through New Mexico late one night, and there were lights all around the car. The compass went crazy, pointing every direction."

"Why is it lucky?"

"I was lucky to have it with me that night," she said.

We sat on a red boulder and watched the setting sun. We get some of the most incredible sunsets in Colorado. The clouds turn orange and purple, and the sun looks like a red ball of fire—which I guess it is. There had been forest fires west of us, and that made the scene even more dramatic. Yellow and pink mixed with the orange and red to create a sight a painter could never dream up.

I told Marion about our trip to the canyon, and she winced and shook her head. "Lots of people have died there, you know."

"You mean drowning in the river?"

"Well, some, yeah, but people die in the Grand Canyon every year, and most of the time they've just been dumb. I have a book that lists the people who've died and why. Some were trying to get a good picture and fell over the railing. One slip and you fall hundreds of feet."

"Don't worry. No way I'm getting close to the edge."

"But you said your mom wants to hike into the canyon."

"One of the side canyons. It's for a book she's working on and—"

"Take plenty of water," she said. "The canyon can reach 120 degrees, and there's little shade. People go crazy and make stupid decisions. Plus there're scorpions, black widows, brown recluse spiders, rattlesnakes—"

"Okay, okay, we'll be careful," I said.

"—killer bees, fire ants, Gila monsters, coral snakes—"

"I get it!"

Marion scooted closer, like she was going to tell me her deepest, darkest secret. "One of my cousins went camping in the canyon a couple summers ago. It was late at night, but the temperature was still about 100. So she's in her sleeping bag, sound asleep, when she hears someone whisper her name. She thinks it's just the wind, so she goes back to sleep. A few minutes later she hears it again, and she sits up. The whispering sounds like her dad's voice."

"I'm not sure I like this story."

"It's totally true."

"That's why I don't like it." I could almost feel the hot wind blowing through the canyon.

"The whisper *was* her father's, and when she moved toward him, she heard him say, 'Stop.' She went back for her flashlight, but even before she got back there, she heard the rattle."

"A snake?"

She nodded. "And not just any snake. A diamondback. It had slithered onto her dad's chest while he was sleeping. She flicked the light on and gasped, because the rattler's head was right next to her dad's neck, next to his carotid artery."

Marion is the best dissector of frogs in the school, but even I knew that the carotid artery is the main one leading from the heart to the brain. "And . . . ?"

"She told him not to move, that she'd get help. But her dad whispered that there wasn't time. The snake coiled and raised its head."

"Enough, Marion, really."

"No, listen. My cousin got a shovel—"

"She didn't kill her dad by accident. Don't tell me that."

"It was one of those little shovels with the short handle. Anyway, she stuck it out, and the snake struck at the metal part. She got the shovel underneath it and flung the snake away."

"Her dad lived?"

She nodded. "But they never camped in the canyon again."

CHAPTER 5

☻ *Bryce* ☻

Marion's story freaked Ashley out. As she packed the night before we were to leave, she inspected her clothes at least 50 times.

I slipped our family DVD into my backpack, the one with my Little League games and all Ashley's dance recitals. It would be fun to inflict it on her. I packed binoculars, night-vision glasses, all the stuff I thought we might need to make the trip intriguing.

When Sam came to check on us and say good night, I asked if he ever worried that the terrorists would come looking for him.

He shrugged. "They think they killed me. They don't know my new name. Unless I do something really stupid, they'll never know I'm alive."

"What would happen if you ran into that guy who thought up the whole thing?"

Sam looked down and pawed the carpet with his boot. "I don't think I've gone to sleep once since the crash without imagining what I'd do to that guy. Sometimes I wonder where God was when the plane went down. If there is a God, why did he let that happen?"

"I know there's a God," I said, "and I still ask the same question." I'd heard all the explanations, like our life is a quilt and we can only see the underside of it where all the pieces are sewn together, but God sees the finished product from the top. I wish I could say those things helped. "When your dad's dead, even if you have a good stepdad, you feel like something's missing that you'll never get back."

Sam gave me a sad smile. "Sometimes I wonder what your real dad would think of you now. When you and Ashley make a good grade or solve some mystery or are just kind to Dylan or Leigh, I see a little of him shining through. I wish I'd have known him."

Sam stared at my picture of Wrigley Field, the one my real dad bought me. I like the Rockies, but there's a special place in my heart for the Cubs, the team my dad and I shared.

"This is going to be a good vacation for us," Sam said finally. "There's a lot to do on that lake. Plus, the trip into the canyon."

I told him Marion's snake story, and he chuckled. "I don't think your mom knows all the things that can happen down there. I'm sure she wouldn't be taking Dylan if she did, but I'll be there."

PART 2

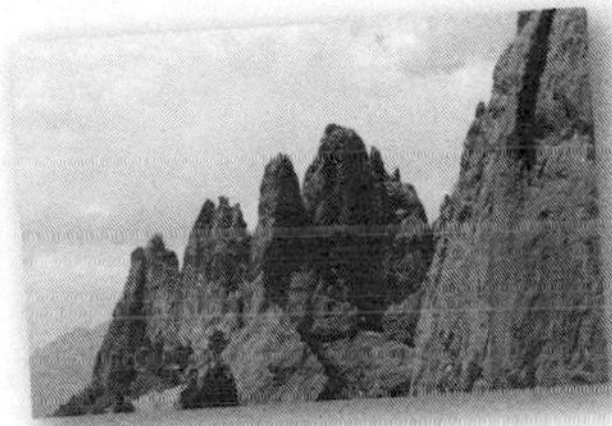

CHAPTER 6

Ashley

Sam had a thermos of coffee, and the smell wafted through the kitchen as I dragged my favorite pillow and blanket to the car.

The lights of our house faded into the early morning fog as we headed for I-25, then turned north toward Denver. A freight train chugged down the tracks near the interstate, and we heard its whistle. I wanted to wake Dylan and show him, but Mom put a finger to her lips. People say let sleeping dogs lie, and I guess that goes for four-year-olds as well.

I fell asleep myself and didn't wake up until we were going through the Eisenhower Tunnel on I-70. My ears popped from the altitude, which is more than 10,000 feet above sea level. When we came out the other side, the sunlight was blinding.

"Hungry," Dylan mumbled.

Mom handed him a blueberry muffin, most of which wound up on my jeans. I let the humming road lull me back to sleep.

I woke up at 10:15 when Sam pulled into a Cracker Barrel. We ate and got back on the road, but before we made it to the interstate, Sam pulled over and bought a dozen ears of corn, boasting that it was the sweetest in the country. I guess he was planning to roast them on the grill on our houseboat.

CHAPTER 7

◐ *Bryce* ◐

I thought about buying corn on the way home and selling it in Red Rock, if it really was as good as Sam said. We'd find out soon enough, I guessed.

The miles rolled by, and we gradually left the mountains and moved into Utah. The scenery was pretty, but the towns were far apart and there wasn't much to them. Signs pointed to Indian reservations, national parks, wilderness areas, and forests. The map showed Bryce Canyon National Park. I thought it would be funny to take a picture and tell our friends it was named after me, but it was out of the way.

"Are we almost there?" Dylan whined.

Mom tried to get him to go back to sleep, but he kept complaining about being hot. Sam turned the air-conditioning up. The temperature gauge on the mirror said 98, but Mom put on a sweater. You can't please everyone.

We finally turned south onto a smaller highway, and it seemed like forever before we saw the water. But when we did, it was incredible. It was like an ocean in the middle of the desert. In the distance limestone formations hovered over the landscape.

We checked into a hotel in a town called Bullfrog, and Sam took us to a restaurant that overlooked the water. We walked along the shore after dinner, and Ashley brought a lake map along. She pointed out several places that looked good to explore and said there were ancient ruins scattered around.

Sam made a phone call, then asked me to go with him on the ferry to the other side to pick up our houseboat. The ferry operator was an older man who looked like he'd lived on the lake all his life. White beard. Yellow teeth. Sweat stains on his shirt.

"Be careful of the crazies," the man said. "College kids. Drink too much, play music all night. When they go out on their Sea-Doos at midnight, it gets noisy."

The man at the marina had huge, hairy arms. He led us onto a dock that moved as we walked. The houseboat was big, but it was scary to step on something and feel it bob up and down.

Sam listened closely as the guy explained every detail about the boat, the generator, and the radio. I went to explore the rooms.

There was a deck on top where you could tan and read a book. A slide led to the water, and it was all I could do to not try the thing out. A sitting area on the back had padded benches, coolers, and a grill. The main room had a big bed, a television, and windows all around. There was also a little bathroom and shower.

Two other bedrooms lay on the other side with a set of bunk beds in each. Through the hall was another bathroom that looked like you'd have to pry yourself in with a shoehorn. Then came the kitchen, complete with refrigerator, stove, and sink. The dining area was nice, with a small table and a bunch of chairs.

The boat was so hot inside I thought I was going to die. I remembered the DVD of white-toothed people and wondered if they'd come some other time of year. This wasn't the same boat we'd seen in the DVD.

Marina Man said something about the air-conditioning, and I sighed with relief. No way Dylan could stand this heat. The thing had to be cooler when it was moving.

The man told Sam the best places for younger families to go. Then he looked out the front window and strung a few bad words together, which made it sound like he'd taken cursing classes and had earned an advanced degree.

Out the window a semi pulled what looked to be the biggest houseboat in history. It was twice the size of ours and looked brand-new. The setting sun glared off the boat's surface.

"There they come," Marina Man said.

"Who?" I said.

"Oh, big shots. Not supposed to say."

"Must be Donald Trump's," I said.

"Probably not far off," Sam said.

A crew backed the big boat into the water, then filled it with fuel. A tall African-American man loaded supplies with the help of a few others, but I didn't see Donald or anyone else who looked rich.

After we loaded our supplies, Sam fired up the engine and we un-hooked the ropes from the dock. As we passed Moby Houseboat, I wondered who in the world would own such a thing.

A curtain opened and a face studied us. A child?

CHAPTER 8

✖ Ashley ✖

Mom and I took Dylan to the gift shop, if you could call it that. They had bait, which made the whole place smell. Dylan wanted everything he saw.

We took him back to the hotel room and let him take a bath. Mom let him play with his cars in the water and poured hotel shampoo in to make bubbles. Dylan gathered them with his hands and put them on his face like a beard, then shaved with his yellow school bus.

I took my diary to the hotel lobby where it was cool and there were big chairs, a pool table, and a big-screen television showing the news.

I curled up and began writing.

> I'm in the lodge, waiting for our houseboat vacation to begin. I'm not sure why, but I feel anxious. I've read about the hiking trails, the weird rock formations, the swimming, boating, and fishing, but something about this whole thing gives me the willies.
>
> What if Dylan falls in while we're not looking? What if some big boat runs into ours and we sink? What if my life jacket doesn't fit? Or what if Marion Quidley is right and there's a Bigfoot around here?
>
> No one else seems worried. Maybe things will get better in the morning.

Suddenly there was a commotion at the front desk. A guy with a bunch of cameras yelled at the clerk behind the counter. "I just want to know when they're getting here!" he said with a British accent.

The clerk picked up a phone, and Camera Guy shoved some money into the man's face. The clerk threw the bills back at him, and soon a manager came to escort Camera Guy outside.

"I'm just doing my job," he said as the manager pushed him through the door.

"Do it somewhere else," the manager said.

CHAPTER 9

◑ *Bryce* ◑

With the houseboat tied up outside, it didn't make sense for all five of us to stay in the same hotel room. It was Ashley's idea that she and I stay on the boat.

Though it was dark, it was still hot outside: At night in Colorado, even in the summer, it actually gets chilly. Here, the temperature was in the upper 80s. A slight breeze helped, and after I unlocked the cabin and showed Ashley around, we opened the bedroom windows and turned on little fans mounted by the beds.

Ashley took the room across from where Mom and Sam would sleep. She unpacked her stuff and folded it neatly in the closet drawers. I threw my suitcase inside the closet and went to see if the TV worked. A couple of stations were fuzzy, so I turned it off. Good thing the boat had a DVD player.

The moon gave enough light to see rock formations in the distance, and lights on the water cast an eerie glow. Music floated to us from the lodge, and people laughed in another boat nearby. I hoped we'd find someplace the next day where we could set up our tent and camp out. Maybe grill some burgers. And corn.

Ashley broke the silence. "What are you thinking?"

"Buying corn. Selling it for a profit."

She rolled her eyes. "Give it a rest."

"We could make some serious cash, Ash."

She shook her head. "I'm worried about Dylan falling in the lake, and you're thinking about making a buck."

"How do you think the guy who owns Moby Houseboat started?" I said, telling her about the big boat. "Small, I'll bet."

Ashley yawned. "I'm going to bed."

She came padding back a few minutes later. "It's too hot."

"Let's move our mattresses up on top."

CHAPTER 10

❈ Ashley ❈

Dragging the mattresses was harder than it looked. The doors to the room were narrow, and the stairs leading to the top deck were even smaller. Bryce had to go up and pull, while I slid the mattress on the handrails toward him. After half an hour we had both mattresses out there, and I was drenched.

Bryce pulled his mattress to one side of the deck, and I stayed on the other. Water lapped at the shore, almost like having your own noise machine to help you sleep.

A bird flew past the moon, and its silhouette made me shudder. Crickets chirped and frogs garumped by the dock. The long drive had made me both restless and tired. Funny how you can sleep most of the day and still be exhausted at night.

"Why do you think Sam chose this place?" Bryce said, his voice lazy like a boat on the water.

"Probably thought it would make up for it if the Grand Canyon bored us."

"I don't think so. Did you see how upset Leigh was that we were coming here?"

She *had* been a little over the top. Like there was something more to this than just a vacation.

"Maybe she just loves heatstroke," I said.

That made Bryce laugh, which made me feel good. It's one thing to make a friend laugh or even a parent, but a brother is the toughest audience.

I lay on my back, studying the stars and thinking about our dad and what it would be like to have him with us. Soon Bryce was breathing deeply, rhythmically.

Footsteps approached on the hill leading from the lodge. I lifted my head. Lights illuminated someone's feet, but I couldn't see a face.

Footsteps on the planks of the dock.

I put my head back on the pillow and closed my eyes.

Footsteps close to our boat.

I held my breath and wished Bryce would wake up.

"Ashley?"

It was Sam. I sat up.

"You okay?"

"Yeah. We brought the mattresses up here because—"

"It's okay. I was gonna suggest that." He looked around, surveying the dock and the boats. "Just making sure you're all right."

CHAPTER 11

◉ *Bryce* ◉

I woke up shaking. I had dreamed Marion Quidley had pledged her undying love to me and wanted to seal it with a kiss. My mouth felt dry, and I'd never wanted a drink of water so bad in my life. But the water was down in the refrigerator.

I lay there staring at the moon. It had moved over us and was on the other side of the lake. I had done a report in third grade about the first person walking on the moon. It didn't seem that big a deal now that we have space shuttles and exploration, but it must have been something in the 1960s.

I tiptoed to the main cabin. The water tasted so good I drank two bottles. Then I needed to go to the bathroom. I had to squeeze in there. It felt about as big as the bathroom on an airplane. Dylan would be fine, I thought, but I couldn't imagine adults in there.

I heard a noise outside, but the window was cloudy so nobody could see in. It sounded like a car had pulled all the way to the dock, but there was no road down here. Then a shadow passed the window—a huge shadow that blocked the moonlight. It was a good thing I had just gone, if you know what I mean. That would have scared it out of me.

I rushed to the back, trying not to make noise. Two headlights shone in my eyes, as if someone were breaking in.

Moby Houseboat glided through the water to my left. That had to have been the shadow that had passed the window. The boat dwarfed everything around it.

The African-American man I had seen on the other side of the lake waved at someone onshore. A radio squawked, and he said something into it. A car door opened, and I knew I had to get topside with Ashley.

When I shook her awake, I put my finger to my lips and pointed at Moby Houseboat. Several people made their way across the dock toward the boat. They held something over their heads—towels?

A guy and a girl were in front, shuffling, with three guys behind, pushing them and looking around. "I can't see their faces," I whispered, "but it doesn't look like Donald Trump."

"Bryce! One of those guys has a gun!"

"You think they're kidnapping the couple?"

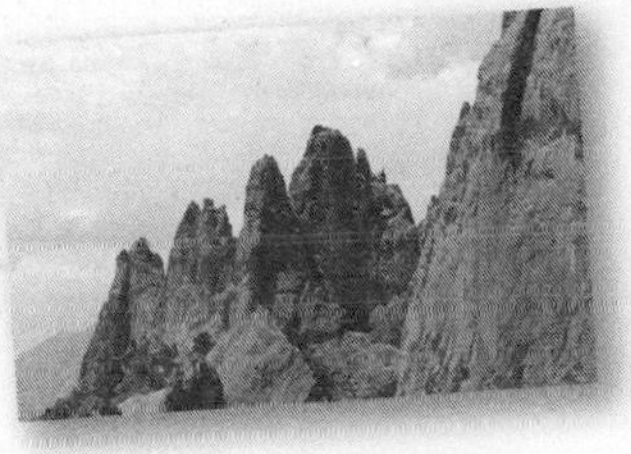

CHAPTER 12

❦ Ashley ❦

It was almost 3 a.m. when Bryce and I scurried onto the dock in just T-shirts and shorts. No way I was going to sleep until we figured this out. Lights were on and music played inside. Weird, if they were kidnappers, unless they were trying to drown out people's cries.

We crept closer on the wobbly dock. Water lapped gently below us. A smaller boat sat directly behind us. We kept going, trying to see in the windows, but the curtains were drawn.

We knelt, wondering what to do. A faint whirring and a *click, click, click* came from the boat behind us.

A child screamed, "Mommy!"

Bryce tensed and I wondered if he was going to jump aboard.

"I saw a face looking out earlier," he said. "It looked like a little kid."

"We have to do something," I said.

Bryce hopped onto a ladder on the side of the boat. "I'm going to have a look."

An explosion of flashes made the scene look more like daytime than night, and I wasn't sure what had happened. A steady, machine-gun fire of flashes.

Someone yelled for everyone to get down. The child wailed. An African-American man above us cursed and pulled a gun.

"Into the water," Bryce whispered, grabbing my wrist and pulling me down. Before I knew it, we bobbed beside the wooden dock. I gripped it and held on. The water was cool, and I thought this was the best decision we'd made all night.

The man with the gun waved it toward the boat behind us. Someone inside laughed and taunted him until he went inside.

Bryce said, "We'd better get out of here or Moby Houseboat is going to—"

The houseboat fired up its engines. Water churned around us and went in my mouth. We had to move.

CHAPTER 13

☻ *Bryce* ☻

The engine of the big boat was so strong it was sucking us under. I hung on to Ashley with one hand and grabbed the dock with the other. Moby spouted water like an angry killer whale. It was barely clear of the dock when it sped out into the lake, missing us by inches.

White light flashed behind as waves crashed into us, making us bob like wet leaves on the surface. I helped Ashley up, then crawled onto the dock, water pouring from my clothes.

Someone came onto the deck of the other boat, hands on hips.

"You kids okay?" the man said with a funny accent. He had short, curly hair and wore a sweat-stained T-shirt.

"That's the camera guy I saw in the lodge," Ashley whispered.

"We're okay," I said. "Just wet. What was that all about?"

"Get back to your boat. Your parents will be hacked off if they find you out here."

I hate it when strangers act like parents. Why couldn't he just answer a simple question?

Seconds after we walked away, his boat zoomed off too.

We toweled off and changed, but going back to sleep wasn't an option. We kept a lookout for either boat. Ashley turned on one of our favorite CDs and kept it low as we watched the sunrise, all red and orange.

"You think those guys are paparazzi?" she said.

"Paparazzi, mamarazzi, brotherrazzi, or sisterrazzi, I don't know," I said. "All I know is they took about a hundred pictures in three minutes. Must be someone special on Moby Houseboat."

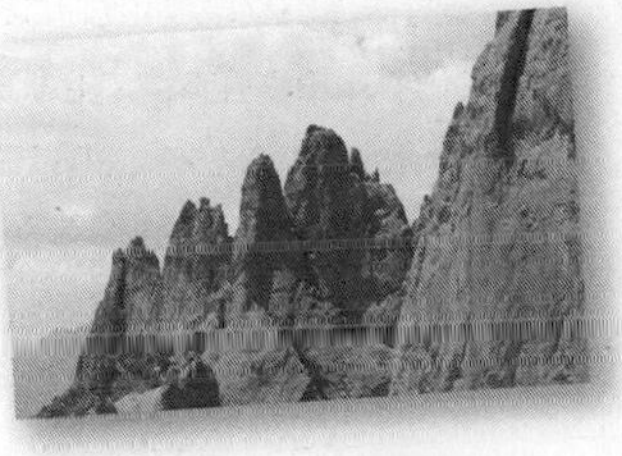

CHAPTER 14

❀ Ashley ❀

"Where should we go this mornin'?" Sam growled, leaning over a map.

Bryce turned it over and pointed to a largemouth bass. "I want to catch 50 of those."

Dylan had his favorite blanket wrapped around his shoulders. He pointed to a crayfish. "I want to catch that."

The map was ringed with pictures of narrow canyons, ancient rock carvings and petroglyphs, and dramatic deep-water rock formations.

Sam showed us where we were, close to the middle of the lake, in Bullfrog Bay. "Let's do some exploring first," he said.

I picked a place called Last Chance Bay, way to the south. Bryce picked a spot to the north named Narrow Canyon.

Sam laughed. "Your choices are about 200 miles apart."

"How about this?" Mom pointed to a little inlet near us called Forgotten Canyon. "I want to see those pictographs."

Sam agreed, and I thought I was going to be sick. If we went only where he and Mom wanted, this was going to be one long trip.

We all donned our life jackets and pulled out. The waterway was surrounded by hill after hill, then broad, flat mesas. To the north stood three mountain peaks.

Already speedboats with water-skiers were tuning up for the day. Several boats sat at the south edge of the bay near sandy beaches. Tents dotted the beach, and smoke rose from campfires. I gestured at rock formations to get Dylan's attention. If he saw sand, he'd want to spend the rest of our vacation digging to China.

Within minutes we were in the middle of spectacular scenery. Lake Powell is a rock lover's paradise—huge rock arches, red rock as smooth as glass, and canyons that look like rock monsters lurking above you.

"Wow," Dylan said.

"Yeah, wow," I said.

CHAPTER 15

☾ *Bryce* ☾

Gazing at rocks all day is not my idea of a good time, no matter how interesting they are. I went to the back of the boat, pulled out the fishing gear, and put a lure on a line.

Fishing is not really Sam's thing. I remember going fishing with my real dad in a little pond close to our house. We'd sit on the bank and watch the bobbers float. Mosquitoes buzzed around us, and he'd point out hummingbirds and animals on the hillside. I don't think we ever caught more than two or three fish, but that still made me love fishing.

I found Forgotten Canyon on another map, and at the bottom it said, "Good fishing spots along the bank."

Forgotten Canyon, here I come.

I climbed to the top of the boat and sat under the canopy with the map and bottled water. Already the temperature had soared, and I could see why we carried so much water.

The map had mile markers beginning in Arizona at the Glen Canyon Dam. We were at mile 106 upstream when we turned into a canyon with sheer rock walls flecked with green.

Mom came topside and just stared at the rocks. "Isn't this something?"

My eyes trolled the water for fish, but I could tell Mom was in book mode. She gets this look in her eyes like she's trying to figure out how she would describe scenery or the look on someone's face. I guess it's kind of like a painter—only she uses words instead of paint.

At the mouth of the canyon a floating sign read:

Forgotten Canyon
   Difficult to spot in the shadows of Forgotten and Moki Canyons are prehistoric Indian ruins.
   Defiance House is 3 miles up this canyon.

The farther we went, the less I understood the name Forgotten Canyon, because it looked like everybody and their brother had remembered it. We finally stopped near a trail that led up the hill to the ruins. I told Mom I wanted to stay and fish, but she begged me to come along.

CHAPTER 16

❀ Ashley ❀

It was a challenge to keep up with Dylan, and we reached the top of the incline before I knew it. We found ourselves behind a group gathered around a guide. The man's voice echoed off the walls.

"About 11,000 years ago," he said, "when prehistoric Indians roamed the Glen Canyon area, mammoth, longhorn bison, and camels shared the land. As the climate changed from cool and wet to hot and dry, these people had to travel to search for food.

"During the Pueblo period, these Native Americans lived in cliffs, building in and around the rock formations to form small dwellings. The Anasazi culture used the rocks and mud to make pottery, baskets, and tools. What you see here is known as Defiance House. The Anasazi were here sometime in the 1200s, perhaps as late as 1280 or 1290 AD."

Behind him stood a small redbrick hut. Around it was a ledge built right on the rocks. I couldn't imagine living in such a place. When the man said the Anasazi people suddenly disappeared and no one knew why, I figured they had found nicer houses with more comfortable furniture.

Sam, Mom, and Bryce joined us as the man pointed out the pictograph on the rock wall showing three warriors with shields and swords. Their legs were funny because it looked like they were squatting as they fought.

"Defiance House was discovered in the late 1950s by a team from the University of Utah. They found two perfect red bowls with scraps of food still in them."

"Yum," Bryce whispered. "And we thought Mom's cooking was bad."

"They named this site Defiance House because of this pictograph, or rock painting."

"Why would they build a house so hard to get to?" someone in the group asked.

The guide shrugged. "We're open to ideas."

"Maybe they wanted to warn their enemies that they'd fight," an older man said.

"Maybe this was just a vacation spot, and they wanted privacy," Bryce said.

The guide chuckled. "Archaeologists have studied these ruins and the markings on the rocks for years. Unfortunately, your guess is as good as ours."

CHAPTER 17

☺ *Bryce* ☺

Mom made lunch as Sam piloted us north about 10 miles to Good Hope Bay. "Want to drive awhile?" he said.

My eyes must have gotten really big. I sat and buckled in.

Dylan squealed, "Bryce is driving! Bryce is driving!"

This was the next best thing to fishing. Sam showed me the controls and reminded me to keep an eye out for stuff in the water. "Propeller can break hitting a tree limb. And you want to slow down when you see those buoys."

"Ashley slows down when she sees boys," I said.

Sam chuckled.

A speedboat passed at what seemed like 100 miles an hour.

"They'll catch that guy sooner or later," Sam said, then told me to turn into the waves so we didn't dip left too much.

A computer screen and a keyboard mounted behind the steering wheel showed an overhead view of the lake. Sam made the picture jump, and the image of the water got bigger.

"This is not just a diagram of the lake," he said. "It's really the lake. Those dots are boats." He clicked a few more times and pointed. "See that? It's us."

We could actually pinpoint our own boat, plus see other craft around us. "Awesome!"

CHAPTER 18

❋ Ashley ❋

We found a spot to stop in Good Hope Bay. Dylan peeled off his life jacket and plopped onto the sand. He was in kid heaven.

Sam kept an eye on him from the bow, munching a sandwich and trying to keep Dylan from disturbing people. The boat next to us had what looked like college kids on their last gasp before school started. They played volleyball with rowdy guys on the next boat. They all talked loud, making me wonder if they were drinking.

When one fell in the water, others laughed and used bad language.

Sam got a look on his face and strode to the boat. He had his shirt off and looked strong enough to throw any one of them in the water.

A young guy came over and Sam spoke low.

The guy nodded. "Yeah, sorry. We'll keep it down."

When the girls saw Dylan, they rushed the beach and surrounded him.

"Isn't he cute?"

"Adorable!"

"Hey, little guy, whatcha doin'?"

"What's your name?"

I hate it when people treat kids like puppies, but Dylan lapped up the attention. He showed them his cars and his new road in the sand. The girls cooed like pigeons until the sun got too hot, and they ran back to their boat. Bryce and I took turns going off the slide and splashing in the water. It felt good to finally swim.

Sam came to the boat railing. "Spectacular hiking not far from here. Dylan's gonna need a nap soon. You and Bryce want to hit the trail with me?"

CHAPTER 19

◑ *Bryce* ◑

It seemed too hot to hike, but Sam knew where he was going. Soon we were in a slot canyon, a narrow walkway with rocks looming. It was as if God had carved a stone hallway for us.

The sun didn't hit us here, and the air blew through, making it cool. We went around a sharp bend, and the rocks got smoother. They felt like stone bowling balls. Water dropped from above, and a raven flew overhead.

We came to where clear water pooled. Ashley knelt, put her hands in, and splashed water on her face. "It's so cool."

"Ready to get your feet wet?" Sam said.

I looked at the small opening in the rock a few feet away. "We're going through that?"

"Follow me."

We slogged through the water in our hiking boots, which didn't seem to bother Sam. When we came to another narrow spot he turned and yelled, "Stay right there. Have to get a shot to scare your mother."

He climbed onto a steep ledge and took our picture with his digital camera. He hurried back to show us, and the look on Ashley's face was priceless: a blank stare as she gazed at the rock walls. I didn't look much better, but at least my mouth wasn't hanging open.

"Just a little farther," Sam said.

We climbed out of the water and through an even narrower path with coarse sand under our feet. The rock turned more and more red and had a weird shape, like someone had put it on a clay wheel and made ovals and indentations. A blast of cool air hit us, and I felt goose bumps. Then Sam disappeared behind a wall of water.

Ashley followed into the darkness, and I was right behind her. We found Sam inside a small cave, looking out at the waterfall. Light flickered, and I spotted a thin shaft above us with a pinhole at the very top. On the side of the wall was a drawing of an animal, like a horse.

I pulled out a flashlight and pointed it straight up. The red walls made it look like I was peering down someone's throat.

"How'd you know this was here?" I said.

Sam smiled. "Let's get back."

CHAPTER 20

✖ Ashley ✖

Later in the afternoon we moved down the lake to Ticaboo Canyon, a word in the Paiute language that means "friendly." The guy who named it is buried at the bottom of the lake—weird but true. We floated through a tree-filled gorge and found a place to stay the night. We arrived just in time, because a bunch of boats came behind us.

Sam cooked burgers and sweet corn on the grill. He was right. He may have found the best corn in the US. But when Bryce sidled up to talk corn business, I blew him off.

We were so hungry from the long hike that Bryce and I devoured two burgers and two ears of corn each and still wanted more.

A boat filled with people attending a reunion parked beside us. They weren't as noisy as the college kids, but close.

On the other side was a family with four kids. Mom talked to them and found out they were from California. The boy who was our age seemed oblivious, like he was in his own world.

Bryce and I slept on top of the boat again. By 10 o'clock the campfires were out, and there was no light except little ones inside the houseboats. I'd never seen that many stars and figured I never would again. The heavens stretched from canyon to canyon and made you feel small and unimportant. On the other hand, if you believe that God made us, knew everything about us even before we were born, *and* that he made every star, every planet, all the fish and animals, the mountains and prairies . . . well, you get the picture. Looking at those stars twinkling millions of miles away made me think of how big God is, how powerful, and it made me wonder why he would love us enough to come to earth and die for us. For me.

I felt something deep in my chest, like when you're really sad or really happy. I was both. Grateful that God loved me. Sad that our real dad wasn't here to share this.

I closed my eyes and thought of all my friends in Red Rock who don't know God. Especially Hayley. I prayed God would get through to her somehow.

When I opened my eyes a tiny light moved across the sky. I poked Bryce's arm. "Shooting star!" I said. "My first ever."

It was still going. "Satellite," he said groggily.

It was the last thing I saw before I fell asleep.

CHAPTER 21

☺ *Bryce* ☺

It was still dark when Sam woke me. He put a finger to his lips and motioned for me to get dressed. The temperature had dropped, and a mist rose from the water, but as soon as I got moving I warmed up.

We climbed down the ladder on the back of the boat and untied the inflatable raft trailing us. All the other houseboats were silent and dark. The reunion people had partied until after midnight, Sam said.

He pushed off and rowed to the mouth of the canyon. I was still partly cloudy with a chance of waking when he handed me a pastry. Cherry. I ate it in three bites, then splashed my hands in the water. Even at that hour you could see how clear and clean the water was.

"Where're we going?" I whispered.

He fired up the little motor and chugged along the bank. That's when I noticed the fishing stuff. Sam cut the motor and drifted into an inlet with lots of plants and brush along the side.

"I was talking with one of our neighbors last night about this spot. He gave me a few of these and said the fish would be hungry this morning."

Sam handed me a plastic bag with lots of little fish in it. I recognized them from a sleepover at my friend Kael Barnes's house. His dad likes anchovies on his pizza, and they dared me to try one. To this day I regret it, though everybody thought it hilarious that I had to run to the bathroom. I caught a whiff of the tiny fish and wondered how anyone in their right mind would put them in their mouth.

"The guy I talked to said they've caught all kinds of fish with these. Water goes down to about 75 feet. When the sun comes up the fish go deeper."

"No eyelids," I said. "They're sensitive to light."

Sam handed me a rod with a hook already on the line. I baited the hook and cast it toward the brush.

Fishing is like hunting for hidden treasure. You never know what you're going to get when you throw your line in. You could come out with nothing. Or a tiny fish. Or something really big. Half the fun is the anticipation of what might be lurking in those waters.

I let the line settle until the anchovy sank to fish-breakfast level. Then I slowly brought my rod to one side, then the other, reeling as I tried to imitate an anchovy's movement. I've never been to anchovy school, but I thought I was doing well.

Sam watched, sipping his thermos of coffee. I have to admit I was disappointed when the anchovy came back without a hit, but I cast again and let it sink deeper.

"Ashley and I were wondering," I said. "Have you ever been to this lake before?"

Sam looked like he was about to answer when something hit my line so hard I thought Kael's dad was down there. My rod curved in a U. I was so excited I tried to stand, but the boat wobbled. I sat and let the fish run a little, then turned the reel a couple of times and pulled.

It took only a minute to bring the fish to the surface, but it felt like an hour. It was gorgeous—a striped bass with two fins on top, a black back, and silver sides. Black stripes ran from head to tail, and it had a pure white underbelly.

"That's a keeper," Sam said. I brought it close, and he gripped it and pulled the hook from its mouth. "Could be a five-pounder."

I grabbed another anchovy, which was looking more and more beautiful. It smelled like victory.

"The record for this lake for striped bass is almost 50 pounds," Sam said. "Imagine a fish 10 times this."

"That would be like catching Dylan," I said. "We'd have to get the fish his own boat."

CHAPTER 22

✖ Ashley ✖

Bryce was smiling from ear to ear as he struggled to hold up a stringer with about 10 fish on it.

Dylan ran to the boat, then held his nose. "Yech!"

Bryce and Sam cleaned the fish, which may be the most disgusting thing I've ever seen. Mom kept her distance too and asked Sam to triple bag the catch so the whole boat wouldn't smell like a fish market. Bryce was excited about fish for dinner, but I swore I was going to find a Subway.

Sam drove us north, past more incredible rock formations and around land that jutted out called The Horn. We had gone about

15 miles when we came in sight of Hite Marina. Sam docked and fueled up. He came back with a set of keys.

"What are those for?" Bryce said.

Sam nodded toward a bunch of smaller boats, rafts, and tubes. He pointed to a two-person Sea-Doo.

Bryce looked at me, then back at Sam. "That's for us?"

I sat behind Bryce (who still smelled like a giant striped bass) and held on as we zoomed into the bay. Water sprayed up around us, and as I waved at Mom I noticed Dylan on the front deck of the houseboat crying, reaching for us. I guess he figured he'd never see us again. Mom stood behind him, probably trying to convince him we'd be back.

Bryce turned right into the first canyon and pulled up so Sam could catch us in the houseboat. I asked Mom to throw us some sunscreen. I slathered it on my neck and arms. Then we switched and I drove while Bryce used the sunscreen.

We had gone only a couple hundred yards when Bryce tapped me on the shoulder.

"What?" I said, annoyed.

Bryce pointed to a hidden cove we had passed three times. In the shade of some trees sat a huge white boat.

"There's Moby," he said.

CHAPTER 23

☾ *Bryce* ☾

Sam stopped at a nearby beach. There was space for only a few houseboats, and one was so old it looked like it was ready to sink. A little farther up the beach a few people sat around a foldout table. Dylan wandered toward them and I followed.

The people doted on Dylan. Offered him a marshmallow. There was an older man and woman, along with a younger woman and a bald guy. When Ashley joined us, they found out we were twins, and they stared at us like it was the first time they'd ever seen a pair.

We found out they were the ones in the old boat. Ron and Anne Lester, along with their daughter, Sheila, a redhead. The bald guy was Ricky Burns, Sheila's fiancé.

"Why don't you have any hair?" Dylan said.

I pulled Dylan close to tell him he shouldn't ask questions like that.

Ricky waved it off. "It's okay. He's just curious." He leaned over, his elbows on his knees. "I have a disease, and when they gave me medicine, my hair fell out. But don't worry. You can't get it from me."

Ricky coughed and Sheila picked up the story. "We were going to get married next June, but when Ricky got sick we moved the date up to October. Ricky's dream was to come to Lake Powell and do some fishing. Because of people on the Internet, we were able to take this trip."

"People gave money?" I said.

She nodded. "A reporter in our hometown did an article about him, and a friend started a Web site." She gave us the address and told us how nice people at the hospital had been. "Dr. Boyle has been great. Ricky said he even contributed to this trip. We're so grateful."

"God can help you," Dylan said.

I felt like pulling Dylan back again, but he was right. God does care about people who are sick.

"You must be churchgoers," Mrs. Lester said. "The Lord has been so good to Ricky, even with all his problems."

Ricky asked where we were from and why we were here.

Ashley told them all about our trip, that Mom was a writer, and that we were heading to the Grand Canyon later. She even told them the trail on the canyon we were supposed to take.

The Lesters and Ricky listened, while I scoped out the layout of the canyon. If I was right, Moby Houseboat was on the other side of the bluff behind them.

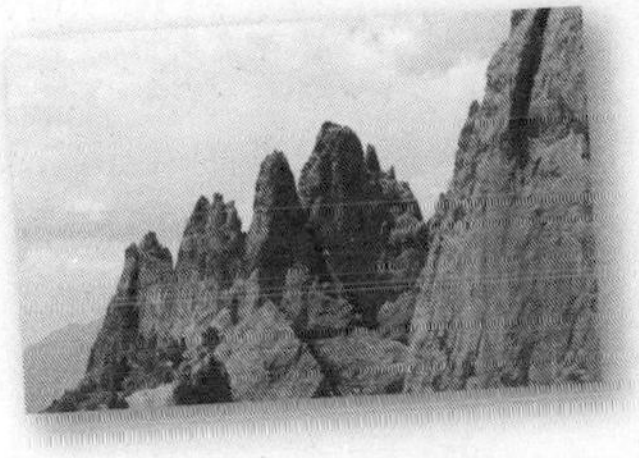

CHAPTER 24

❋ Ashley ❋

After lunch, Bryce and I climbed a steep path to a knoll overlooking the lake. It was a great view, but we couldn't see Moby until we climbed down the other side. Several times we slipped, sending rocks and dirt toward the water.

"There it is," Bryce said as we came to a huge rock that jutted out over the lake.

We lay down and peered over the edge. The massive boat looked like one of those luxury yachts on TV. We could barely see inside, but through the binoculars I noticed leather furniture on the top floor.

"There's somebody," Bryce said. The tall African-American man came on deck and opened a cell phone, but we couldn't hear him.

"I thought cell phones didn't work out here."

"His must be more powerful," Bryce said. "Or it could be a satellite phone."

It was getting hot on that rock, and something was bothering me. I had a creepy feeling, like we were being watched.

I inched forward and looked down. A ledge ran just below the rock, and I saw movement in the dirt. Something brown slithered. I froze as two black eyes stared at me.

CHAPTER 25

☺ *Bryce* ☺

When I heard the rattle and hiss, I knew Ashley was in trouble.

"Stay still," I whispered. "Is he coiled?"

"Yeah."

I peered over the edge. The snake's eyes were locked on my sister. Its tail twitched furiously, making that hideous sound.

"A coiled snake can strike only half its length," I said.

"Thanks, Dr. Science. Now would you do something, please?"

I wanted to remind her that the rattler was more scared of her than she was of it and that a snake strikes only when it feels threatened, but all I could get out was, "He sure looks big."

Ashley's legs shook, and I knew that could scare the snake into action. I waved and clapped. "Over here, snake! Look at me!"

But he didn't take his eyes off Ashley.

I scooped up some loose rocks. "Stay calm. It can sense your fear."

"Then why doesn't he go away?"

I threw the stones but missed the snake. The clattering made him turn his head, so I grabbed Ashley and pulled her from the edge. She yelped when I skinned her elbows on the rock, but she looked grateful when she was finally on her feet.

I moved to the edge, and she caught my arm. "What are you doing?"

"Just want to see if—"

"Let's get out of here!"

Moby Houseboat was still there, and the guy on deck was looking at us.

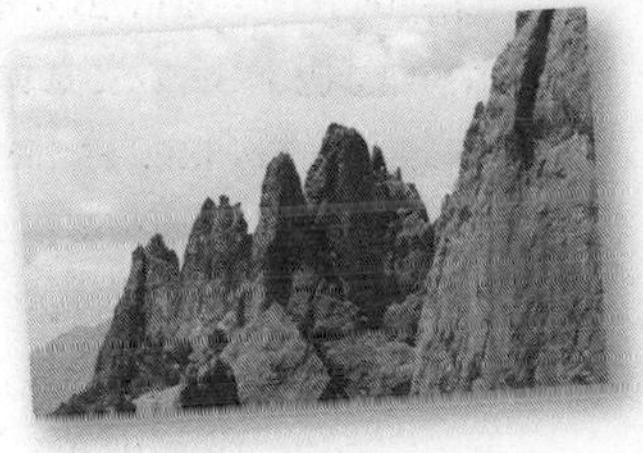

CHAPTER 26

❀ Ashley ❀

Marion's story about the guy with the snake on his chest kept flashing in my mind, and I wondered if I'd have a hard time sleeping.

Why does this stuff always happen to me?

Bryce and I took the Sea-Doo out for a spin. It felt good to be back on the water and out of the reach of anything poisonous. The spray felt good too, because the sun was high.

Bryce drove us to the mouth of the canyon where we could still see our houseboat *and* Moby. Another boat floated nearby.

"Isn't that the one we saw the other night?" I said. "With the weird guy and all the cameras?"

Bryce hit the accelerator, and we did a couple of slow circles around the second boat. It had tinted windows, but I thought I detected movement inside.

Bryce cut the engine and we floated, the water lapping at our feet. I wished they made Sea-Doos with canopies.

Someone onshore ran up the hill, his shirt off. The guy was bald and looked like Ricky.

A door opened on the camera boat, and a curly-haired man smoking a cigarette came outside. He stared at us through sunglasses, leaned against the railing, and flicked the butt into the lake.

I hate it when people make the world their ashtray. "Did you see that?"

Bryce started up the Sea-Doo and drove close to the boat, and I got that sick feeling, like looking at the rattlesnake. Bryce bent over, picked up the cigarette butt, and tossed it back onto the deck. "You dropped this," he said.

The guy smirked. "What are you, Junior Rangers? Lake Patrol?"

"You shouldn't pollute," I said, my voice shaky. "Filters aren't biodegradable."

"Sorry, Officers. I didn't see your badges."

When the man glanced toward Moby Houseboat, Bryce gunned the engine and we spun, spraying the guy. He was shaking his fist and yelling as we sped off.

CHAPTER 27

☺ *Bryce* ☺

It felt good to spray the guy—for about two minutes—then reality set in. What if Curly came after us?

I usually try to think, *What would Jesus do?* Unfortunately, I forgot that time and wound up regretting spraying the guy. Jesus might have called him out for littering, but he wouldn't have drenched him. That was just mean.

I thought about going back and apologizing, but that felt even worse. What if the guy did something to us or our Sea-Doo? There's a saying that you're supposed to let sleeping dogs lie, meaning you shouldn't wake them up, and the more I thought about the guy I'd sprayed, the more he seemed like a sleeping dog—with a camera around his neck, of course.

We rode past our houseboat and farther back into the canyon.

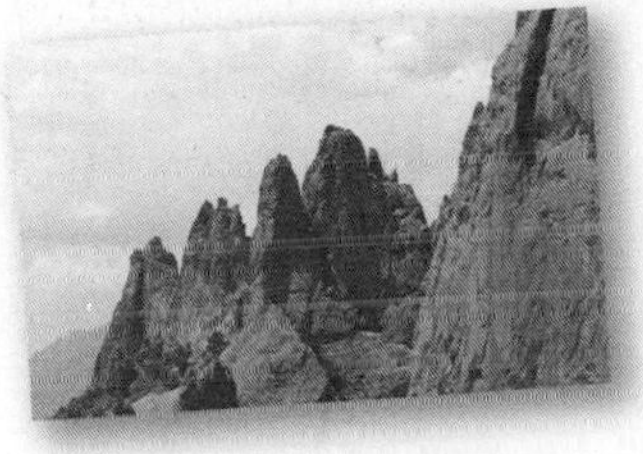

CHAPTER 28

✾ Ashley ✾

We had to return the Sea-Doo, so I wanted to take the fishing raft around The Horn and into the inlet to get a better look at Moby Houseboat. We were loading a couple of rods to make it look convincing when Ricky walked up with his shirt tied around his waist. Sweat beaded on his forehead, and he breathed heavily.

"Looks like you two are going out to catch some dinner," Ricky said.

Bryce told him what he and Sam had caught earlier.

"How are you feeling?" I said.

"Pretty good. This air is great for me."

We paddled close to the shore, and the water was so clear you could see the bottom, like a mountain stream. Bryce got out his fishing line.

Moby was just ahead when we stopped. Trees and shrubs mostly hid it.

"Who do you think is on that thing?" I said.

"Somebody who doesn't mind staying inside," Bryce said. "Haven't seen anybody but that guy with the cell phone."

Bryce made his fishing convincing, casting the line and reeling it in. I kept an eye on the boat and two people on deck.

On the next cast, something made Bryce's line bow. He struggled to get it to the surface, and I kept watching, trying to see what was coming up. When he got it near the surface, Bryce passed his hand through the water, then grabbed and unhooked the fish, and put it back.

"Why'd you do that with your hand?"

"A dry hand takes off some of the fish's scales. If you're going to let it go, you wet your hand and the fish doesn't pick up any bacteria from the skin that could hurt it once it's back in the water. Saw it on a video once."

"Wow, you *are* Dr. Science." I had no idea Bryce knew or cared that much for fish. Of course, I'd just seen him and Sam plunge a sharp knife deep into a bunch of fish bellies, so I knew he was capable of fish butchering, but still . . .

Bryce cast and reeled. He let the line go deep and jerked the rod. "Feels big, but it's not fighting."

A speedboat went by and pushed waves our way. Bryce reeled and brown muck bubbled. He caught the line and pulled out an old boot. I thought it was funny, but then I wondered whose boot it was and whether they were at the bottom of the lake.

Bryce unhooked the boot and dropped it by my foot. "I don't want to pollute the lake."

With all the casting and reeling, the waves pushed us closer and closer to Moby Houseboat. The outside was sleek and white, but I couldn't see much on the deck. I prayed they wouldn't back out and gun the engine. They could easily have flipped us.

Bryce put his fishing pole down and grabbed the oars. He tried to row away from Moby, but the waves kept moving us closer. A tiny voice said, "Hi." I saw a little girl—about Dylan's age—at the railing.

"Hi," I said, waving. "Don't get too close to the edge, okay?"

She moved closer, put a foot on the rail, and pulled herself higher. "What?"

"She's not wearing a life jacket," Bryce said.

"Move back," I said. "Get down and move—"

But it was too late. Her foot slipped and her legs slid through. She screamed and hung on briefly, then plunged toward the lake.

CHAPTER 29

◑ *Bryce* ◑

I was in the water as soon as the girl hit. Ashley yelled for help.

"How did she get by you?" someone screamed. A woman came to the railing, a hand to her mouth.

The girl sank, then bobbed to the surface like I expected. When I reached her she was going under again, gasping and flailing. I grabbed her and tried to keep her head above water, but she gripped my shoulders and pushed me down. I had to get away and grasp her from behind. I wanted to pull her to the back of the boat, but there was no way I could make that. Instead, I pushed her toward the shore.

When I got her onto a rock, she cried and held my neck. Ashley rowed next to us and offered to take the girl to Moby Houseboat, but before we could even learn her name, a motorized boat pulled near us.

It was Curly, the guy with the cameras. I thought he was coming for the girl, but instead of helping us, he shot pictures of us huddled on the bank.

"What are you doing?" I yelled at him.

"My job," he said, snapping shot after shot.

Above us came a scream, and Curly looked up. As I followed his pointing camera, a muscle-bound guy without a shirt dived over the rail. Curly snapped more pictures as the guy hit the water and went under. Curly shouted at the guy near the motor, "Go, go, go! He's coming!"

Curly's boat zoomed backward, and the shirtless guy started treading water. I thought he looked familiar.

Ashley tossed me a towel, and I draped it around the little girl. From behind Moby Houseboat came another motorboat driven by the tall African-American man. He sped up to the shirtless guy and pulled him aboard. Then he came to get the girl.

The woman appeared on the railing and called to her. "Toomer! Are you okay?"

Toomer puckered and wailed, nodding as tears streamed. I handed her to the shirtless guy. He didn't thank me or even acknowledge I was alive.

Curly still held his camera aloft and shot as his boat zipped away. When Ashley helped me into the boat, Curly turned his camera toward us.

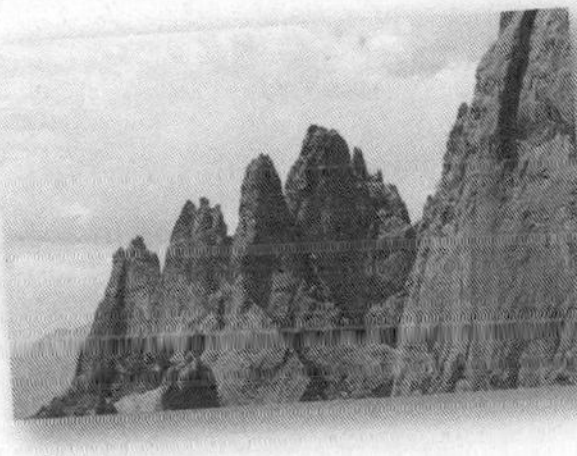

CHAPTER 30

✾ Ashley ✾

"Looks like you took a swim, Bryce," Sam said. "Catch anything?"

"A boot," I said, laughing.

Bryce dried off and changed, and we went to the beach. Most of the houseboats had moved on, and Mom was busy doing some prep work for her book. Mr. and Mrs. Lester came up to Bryce and me.

"You two all right?" Mr. Lester said. "We heard how you saved that little girl's life. Ricky was on the bluff and saw the whole thing. Your parents must be proud."

I looked around to see if Sam or Mom had heard.

Mrs. Lester said, "Ricky says they're rich. The boat's the size of Texas. Guess you met 'em."

"Not to talk to them," Bryce said. "I think I've seen the guy who jumped in the water, but I don't know where."

While Sam was cooking Bryce's fish, Bryce and I went into the cabin to the computer. We pulled up a search engine, and I typed in *Toomer.* Several listings covered a writer and philosopher, another was for a football player, a public school in Atlanta, and then I clicked on a celebrity page.

> *Skylar Maxwell's career stalled after several starring roles. Her marriage to actor Jack Brandon lasted less than five years and produced two daughters, **Toomer** and Rala. She is rumored to be dating tennis star Griffin McElroy, the jewelry-laden star ranked seventh in the world.*

I looked at Bryce. "You don't think that's Skylar and Griffin's boat."

Bryce typed in Griffin's name and pulled up a picture. I had heard his name on the sports news but hadn't paid much attention. When his photo came up, I recognized him as the guy who had jumped in the water.

"That's why those photo hounds are here," Bryce said.

"So that's what happened the first night? They were shooting them while they got on the boat."

Bryce nodded. "Says here Griffin is supposed to be training for the US Open. Funny way to do that. It's in New York."

"Bryce? Ashley?" Sam called. "Somebody out here to see you."

CHAPTER 31

☺ *Bryce* ☺

When I saw the curly-haired photographer, my mouth dropped open and my stomach clenched. It was like seeing Boo Heckler, a bully from our school who's one of the meanest guys on the planet.

Curly smiled at Sam and nodded. "Plucked her right out of the water, sir. Amazing stuff."

Sam turned to me. "You said you didn't catch anything."

"I didn't think humans counted," I said.

Ashley and I stepped off the boat, and Curly stuck out his hand. "Adrian Davis. Nice to meet you." He lowered his voice. "Sorry about the little misunderstanding. You were right about my polluting. Listen, I got good shots of the rescue. Two papers are already offering lots of cash. Give me your name and your story, and I'll make it worth your while."

Sam had told us a long time ago how important it was for us not to publicize pictures of our family—because of his past. But my first thought was *how much?*

"You know who those people on the boat are, right?" he said.

"Think so," I said.

"Hottest couple on the planet." He moved closer. "Griffin and Skylar are looking for you. My guess is they'll ask you to come aboard." He opened his jacket and pulled out a tiny gray camera about the size of a cigarette lighter. "Pictures inside that boat would be worth a fortune."

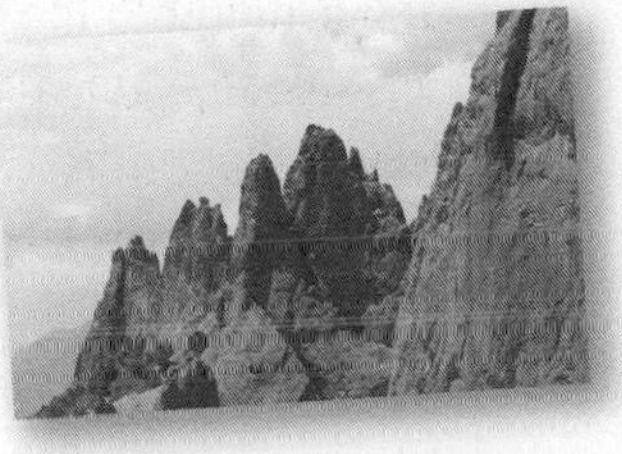

CHAPTER 32

Ashley

I couldn't believe Bryce took the camera. Adrian urged him to use it, told us how to contact him on the radio, then left.

Sam cleared his throat and flipped a fish. He didn't have to say anything.

"I was going to tell you, Sam," Bryce said. "But I was afraid you wouldn't let us go out alone again."

"Why would I do that? You saved a kid's life."

"We *were* kind of spying on that big boat," I said.

"Why? You knew who was on it?"

"No." We explained what we'd seen the first night.

Sam adjusted the heat under the fish and stuck out his lower lip.

As we talked a speedboat rushed in from the bay with one person aboard, the tall African-American man from Moby Houseboat. He scanned the beach with binoculars and stopped when he saw Bryce and me.

Just then Ricky walked up. He patted Bryce on the shoulder. "I saw the rescue. Good job."

I felt sorry for Ricky with his disease and all, but I wished he would go away. Instead, Sheila joined him. "Fish smells good," she said. "What do you put on that?"

Sam told her. Bryce and I moved to the railing when the man in the speedboat pulled alongside. He had short black hair and a goatee. He was all business, staring with intense eyes.

He introduced himself as Terrance. "My employer wants to thank you," he said. "How many in your family?"

Bryce told him.

"I'm authorized to invite all of you to dinner on my employer's boat." He looked at Sam. "Bring the smaller boat and dock near the rear deck."

"You don't need any fish, do you, Terrance?" Sam said.

It was as close to a smile as we got out of the man. "In an hour? Seven?"

CHAPTER 33

☻ *Bryce* ☻

"*Leigh will kill us,*" Mom said. "She loves Skylar's movies."

We piled into the small boat, and Sam buzzed around the cove. Two smaller boats stood guard. The pilots studied us, then waved Sam through.

Terrance led us into the main cabin and seated us in leather chairs. Music played in the background—guitars and strings—and I recognized one of my favorite movie soundtracks. I expected posters and tennis gear, but there was none of that. They did have a huge plasma-screen TV and two rows of DVDs.

A girl in a bright orange swimsuit and life vest bounced into the room. She had pigtails, a wide smile, and Barbie sandals. I guessed this was Rala. When she saw us, her eyes grew wide and she ran back out. A lady led her back in by the hand, along with Toomer. When Toomer saw me she smiled and hid behind her mom's long sundress.

"I'm Skylar," she said, holding out her hand to Sam and Mom. "This is Rala." She looked at me. "And I think you've already met Toomer."

I smiled and nodded, which was all I could think of. The two girls sat next to Skylar like frightened pups. I wondered whether Skylar was really this nice, or if this was just another role.

It's hard to know how to treat really famous people, but Skylar didn't seem too impressed with herself. She didn't wear much makeup and wasn't wearing glitzy clothes like you see on *Entertainment Tonight.* I was thinking what a regular person she was when a guy handed her a piece of paper and she took our orders for her personal chef.

"Toomer," Skylar said, "why don't you show Ashley the boat? I bet she'd like to see it."

"I want to go too," Dylan said.

That sent Rala and Toomer into a competition for Ashley. Luckily, she has two hands. They dragged her down the stairs with shouts of, "I want to show her my room first!" Dylan raced after them.

Skylar leaned forward. "You probably think I'm a really bad mom."

"Believe me," Mom said, "with Dylan on board, I know it's easy to lose track."

Skylar looked at me with her blue eyes, and my hands went clammy. I didn't want to stutter, so I just kept my mouth shut.

"I wanted to thank you for what you did for Toomer," she said.

"Griffin heard the splash and dived right in after her, but you were already there."

I shrugged. "It wasn't that big of a deal."

"Of course it was. I can't imagine what would have happened. . . ." She put a hand to her face, and her voice grew thick. "I just want you to know how grateful I am, and if there's anything I can do for you, let me know."

CHAPTER 34

※ Ashley ※

The boat didn't feel like a boat at all. It looked like a product of *Extreme Makeover: Boat Edition.* Rala had a princess theme, complete with a castle bed built into the wall. Toomer's was a cheerleader design with lots of pictures of hunky guys on the wall, which seemed strange for someone her age.

"Let me show you Griffin's office," Rala said.

"Maybe we'd better not," I said, but she ran ahead and burst into the room.

"Rala, I told you not to—" Griffin looked up and saw me.

"I'm sorry," I said. "She was showing me her room and—"

"You helped Toomer today," he said, standing. He closed the lid of a wooden box. The first thing I noticed was the jewelry around his neck. "It's okay. I'm glad you're here. It's probably time for dinner."

He came out from behind the desk, and I couldn't help staring. He looked like a bronze statue. He shook my hand, and I told him my name. I don't think I've ever seen teeth so white.

"Nice to meet you, Ashley. Sorry I didn't have time to talk with you today."

Stir-fried vegetables and steak wafted through the hallway, and I couldn't wait.

The table was set like one of those fancy restaurants, and I was sure Dylan would bump it and the whole thing would crash. But Skylar showed Dylan, Toomer, and Rala to a specially made picnic table with plastic cups, plates, and forks.

"The deck is locked," Skylar told Mom.

Bryce gave me a look when he saw how much silverware there was. We both get nervous when there's more than a knife and fork.

A woman in a uniform served us salad, shrimp cocktails, strawberry lemonade (with real strawberries), and then our choice of salmon, steak, or chicken, along with the stir-fried vegetables.

"Next year we have to get this boat," Mom said, chuckling.

I worried what to talk about, but our hosts took care of that. We talked about them. Skylar was between films. The US Open was coming up at the end of the month, and Griffin was taking some time to relax.

"Why'd you pick Lake Powell?" Sam said.

Griffin shrugged. "We could have gone to some island, but we get mobbed and it's pretty far. A friend of Skylar's offered us the boat and said if we kept quiet about it, we might not be followed." He looked out the window. "No such luck. The price of fame. Sometimes I wish we could live like regular people."

"We'll trade boats," Bryce said, and everybody laughed.

"Your children have beautiful names," Mom said.

Skylar frowned. "Most people think I'm weird for giving them those names. Toomer is named after a writer my mother loved. *Rala* is a word Toomer used to say when she was younger. It means happy. At least, it did to Toomer."

Skylar touched her head and said she wasn't feeling well. It might have had something to do with the noise Dylan, Toomer, and Rala were making in the children's wing.

"We need to head back anyway," Sam said. "But this has been great. Thanks so much."

Griffin put a hand on Bryce's shoulder. "I was thinking about what you said about switching boats. One thing I've wanted to do since I came here is to hike to the corkscrew. No way I can with those camera hounds. You guys want to hike it with me?"

"Sure!"

He told us what radio channel to use to talk with him. "Come back early in the morning, and I'll sneak onto your boat. Your mom and little brother can switch places with me. Then we'll head out. We'll call this Operation Corkscrew."

CHAPTER 35

☮ *Bryce* ☮

Ricky and the Lesters had to hear all about the dinner as we joined them at the campfire. Ricky was most curious about the boat itself.

"I've seen Skylar's movies," Mrs. Lester said. "She's known as a party girl. Sounds like she's trying to settle down."

"Wish I could play tennis like that Griffin guy," Ricky said. "Beats working at the factory."

"Can you imagine all that money?" Mr. Lester said. "Don't know what I'd do with it."

When we told them we were going hiking into the corkscrew

with Griffin, Ricky shook his head. "Wish I could go." He coughed. "I'm just not feeling well. Maybe too much sun."

Sheila pulled his baseball cap off and rubbed his head. "You can sleep all day tomorrow and be as good as new. Supposed to rain anyway."

Ashley and I slept atop the boat again that night, watching the stars and talking. "You still have Adrian's camera?" she said.

"Yeah, I used it a few times on Moby Houseboat."

"You didn't!" she said, sitting up in her sleeping bag.

"Want to see the pictures?"

I flipped open the small digital camera and showed Ashley how to scroll through. The first picture was Ashley stepping onto the houseboat and almost falling. The second was her putting stir-fry in her mouth with the wrong fork. The third was her coming out of the bathroom, and I took one more from behind her with Griffin, Skylar, and her kids waving from the deck.

"Bet the tabloids will pay big bucks for these," she said, snorting.

"All I have to do is get them to Adrian, and we're rich."

"Seriously, you'd never—"

I shook my head. "'Course not. I don't know why I took it from the guy. I'll erase those and get it back to him before we leave."

"You might want to save this one," Ashley said. "Look behind the boat, up on the rock where we saw the snake."

It was tiny, but I could make out a face looking from the rock. Someone had been watching us.

CHAPTER 36

❀ Ashley ❀

I awoke to the smell of sizzling bacon, which helped me shake off a snake dream. Sam had made eggs and toast too, and my stomach growled.

Bryce studied the weather forecast on the boat's computer.

Partly cloudy with isolated showers and thunderstorms late morning. Scattered showers and thunderstorms in the afternoon. Highs near 100. Chance of rain, 50 percent.

"Same forecast as yesterday and it didn't rain at all," Bryce said.

After breakfast Bryce tuned the radio to the right channel and keyed the mike. "Calling Moby. This is the good ship Timberline requesting permission to come alongside."

A man answered. "Granted."

I counted seven boats near the big white one, but these guys were fishing for pictures.

As soon as we pulled up, one of the guards, wearing a dark jacket, baseball cap, and sunglasses, stepped onto our boat. I soon realized it was Griffin.

Once he was out of sight of the photographers, Mom took his jacket, sunglasses, and hat, put them on, and carried Dylan onto Moby.

"Let's go before those weasels catch on," Griffin said.

Sam fired up the boat and pulled away. The photographers didn't catch on, and we passed them without problem. Bryce saw Adrian, the guy who gave him the camera, and waved it at him. Griffin stayed hidden inside Sam and Mom's room until we were a safe distance away.

We motored south toward Antelope Canyon, past the Utah/Arizona border. Griffin finally moved to the front and asked Sam what he did for a living. Sam gave him the bare bones.

Griffin sat up. "I'm looking for a full-time pilot. Interested?"

Sam smiled. "It's better for me and the family to stay freelance. If I worked for you, I'd have to base out of one place—"

"We could work it out. I'd pay you top dollar."

"I'm sure you would," Sam said.

We passed Last Chance and Padre bays and saw Tower Butte in the distance. We were close to the Colorado River now, just past the dam. That leads through the Grand Canyon, which I was increasingly not looking forward to. We passed Antelope Island, and Sam pointed out Navajo Canyon and the northern perimeter of the Navajo Indian Reservation, the largest in America.

When Griffin went to get something to drink, I saw my chance.

"Have you noticed anybody up on the rocks behind your boat watching you?"

He shrugged. "That's what I have bodyguards for."

I showed him the picture Bryce had taken of the face in the rocks.

"Probably paparazzi," he said.

CHAPTER 37

☯ *Bryce* ☯

Sam held down the fort at the boat while Ashley and I followed Griffin into the canyon. I knew immediately why he was such a great tennis player. He used an economy of steps, picking his spots, jumping from one rock to another, his legs propelling him. Ashley and I were out of breath just trying to keep up.

"If my agent knew I was doing this, he'd kill me," Griffin yelled. "A sprained or twisted ankle would put me out of the tournament."

"So why are you?" Ashley said.

"Because I can!"

The scenery changed, and we found ourselves in the middle of a steep canyon. Clouds formed and the sky grew dark. I wasn't worried about lightning, because there were a lot of caves to crawl into or ledges to get under. Ashley kept scanning the ground, I guess for snakes.

We came to a steep gully with a little water in it. Griffin hollered at us to keep going. He was literally walking with one foot on either side of the canyon, inching along above the water.

Ashley and I followed, walking the same way. It was easy until our legs got tired, and we had to step in the water. I don't like wet socks, but the water cooled our feet.

The rock turned orange-red and rose with smooth ridges. I'd seen postcards in gift shops with views like this, but I never thought I'd actually see a real one.

When it began sprinkling the rocks grew slick. Griffin was now so far ahead that we'd lost him.

"What if somebody kidnaps him?" Ashley said.

"He'd probably love it," I said.

CHAPTER 38

✖ Ashley ✖

After a few minutes of yelling for Griffin, I got worried. What if he'd fallen into some chasm?

I screamed when he jumped out of a cave and nearly scared me to death. He roared laughing and loped ahead again.

The rain came heavier now, and water cascaded down the canyon. It was pretty the way water changed the colors of the rock. We followed a ledge to the top of a mesa, where Griffin looked at a map and pointed. "I think it's that way—yeah, you can see the railing to the stairs."

Athletes are supposed to be in good shape, but Griffin was ridiculous. His legs were nothing but muscle and bone, and he moved like a cat.

The first rumble of thunder made him duck. He looked back with wide eyes. "I don't like that."

Bryce and I didn't either and began moving more cautiously.

The rain fell straight and drenched our hair and clothes. I tilted my head back, and the rain on my tongue tasted heavenly. I wished Hayley could be here.

We finally made it to the canyon and found we were alone. A plaque read:

> *In memory of those who lost their lives in a flash flood*
> *August 12, 1997*

Eleven names were listed with their ages and where they were from—seven from France, one from England, one from Sweden, and two from the USA. The youngest had been 10 years old. The oldest was 45.

"Come on, let's go down!" Griffin called from the top of the stairs.

CHAPTER 39

☺ *Bryce* ☺

The plaque gave me the creeps. Those people had just been out for fun like us. They'd had no idea their lives would end that day.

What had they talked about as they walked along? Had the 10-year-old complained about the heat? the rain? Were the people together when the water rushed them?

The back of my right foot really hurt, so I sat on the stairs and pulled my shoe and sock off. I found a big blister on my heel.

"Hold up down there," I hollered, my voice echoing off the smooth walls. I stuck a Band-Aid over the blister, put my shoe and sock back on, and headed down.

I had to hold the railing as we went into the corkscrew, a hole in the rock that winds down and down through walls that look like sand dunes. I was glad we didn't have to climb the rocks. That would have taken hours.

Griffin and Ashley waited at the bottom, and just as we turned, the sun came out and a shaft of light lit the scene like God's spotlight. It was the most incredible thing I'd ever seen.

"Wish I had a camera," Griffin said.

I pulled out the one Adrian had given me.

"Nice," he said.

"You wouldn't believe where it came from," Ashley said.

Griffin pointed to a ledge. "You guys stand there."

We climbed into place, and he clicked the shutter a couple of times.

"Let me get one of you," I said.

Griffin stood on the ledge with Ashley and smiled. What had his parents had to put up with when he was a kid? Lessons. Tournaments. Tantrums. Sam and Mom probably had it easy compared with Griffin's mom and dad.

I took a picture and was about to snap another when I heard something roar and gush, like a gust of wind coming toward us.

Griffin's mouth dropped. "Flash flood!"

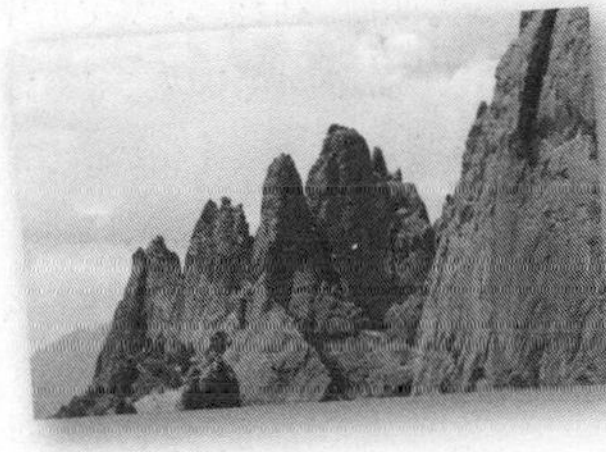

CHAPTER 40

❀ Ashley ❀

My heart pounded as we raced for the stairs. Water gushed through the canyon while we clawed our way to the metal railing. Griffin helped me up, and I used the rails to jump two steps at a time. Bryce bounded to the steps just as a surge of water washed past us. The three of us reached the top and sat on the ledge watching the water roar through the canyon.

"No wonder those walls look so polished," Bryce said.

Griffin scratched his chin. "How did all that water get here so fast? It's not raining that hard. That must be why they built the stairs. It could be dry here and raining a couple of miles away. The water builds up and takes people by surprise."

"Kind of like lightning on Pikes Peak," I said. "It can be clear and no clouds and you can be struck."

It took a long time to make it back to the lake because Bryce was limping so much. Even Griffin looked shaken. I just wanted to get back, have some dinner, and crawl into bed with my diary. It had been one of those kinds of days.

CHAPTER 41

☺ *Bryce* ☺

Dry socks are wonderful. I changed as soon as we got to the boat. Griffin called Skylar on his satellite phone and told us dinner would be ready when we got back. But I couldn't wait. I opened a bag of chili-cheese corn chips and a couple of sodas.

Ashley wouldn't talk about the hike. I guess the flash flood had shaken her, especially after seeing that plaque. She threw an inner tube off the back of the boat, and Sam slowed long enough for her to swim to it. We pulled her behind the boat through waves kicked up by speedboats and skiers. It looked fun, but there was no way I was going to risk infection by soaking my foot in that water.

She finally pulled herself back to the boat. "Notice something different about Griffin?" she said when we were alone. "He's not wearing a hundred pounds of jewelry."

Griffin stuck his head into the cabin. "But I'm putting it back on soon."

Ashley's face flushed. "I'm sorry. I didn't mean to—"

"It's okay," Griffin said, smiling. "I know people think it's weird, but I like it. It's my thing—and I get more media attention because of it. In fact, I just bought something I'll show you when we get back. The US Open crowd is gonna love it."

"I can't wait," Ashley said.

"And, Bryce," he said, "let me show you a trick with that blister. I've had my share."

The blister had filled with fluid and was puffy. Griffin found a safety pin, lit a match, and held the flame under the metal for a few moments, then stuck the pin in the white skin and pushed the fluid out.

"If you tear the dead skin off it heals slower. Better to leave it as a covering. Put a couple of Band-Aids over it, and you'll be back in business."

I thanked him but didn't have the heart to tell him I already knew that. I wanted to tell him about our own tennis experience, but I figured he wouldn't care.

By the time we reached Moby Houseboat, I was so full of chili-cheese corn chips I could hardly move. A few more photographers' boats had been added to the fleet, and Griffin just waved as we passed.

Adrian yelled at someone beside him, and another guy smacked a baseball cap against the boat railing.

Mom met us at the back of the boat with Dylan. Skylar stayed inside, out of range of the cameras. The chef cooked some of my catch from the day before, and I really regretted eating all the corn chips.

We were settling down to dinner when Griffin ran in with a look of horror. "Did you move my new necklace, Sky? The one in the wood box?"

"I didn't touch it."

He looked at Rala and Toomer. "Did you girls see my necklace?"

Toomer looked up. "Maybe that guy took it."

Skylar turned. "What guy?"

"He said not to tell anyone."

Griffin's gaze darted back and forth. He called for Terrance. "Call the police."

CHAPTER 42

❀ Ashley ❀

I could see the wheels turning in Griffin's mind. Who could have stolen his precious necklace? One of the photographers? Somebody on his own staff? Us? Toomer couldn't describe the man because she said he wore a rubber suit and mask.

Skylar had let the security guy and the chef go to the marina for supplies, and they had been gone almost the whole day. Skylar and Mom hadn't seen anyone come aboard, but they had stayed in the living area, away from the office.

Bryce went back to our boat and loaded his photos into the computer, then gave Griffin the tiny camera. "Maybe the cops can enlarge the picture that shows the guy's face."

As we were leaving, a boat with a flashing red light pulled up to Moby Houseboat.

"What's going on over there?" Adrian yelled.

"Nothing to speak of," I said.

Adrian shook his head. "C'mon! Give me something!"

We drifted up to the sand, and Sheila arrived to ask how we were. I told her about the flood, and she seemed genuinely concerned.

"Where's Ricky?" I said.

"Inside," Sheila said.

"Has he been there all day?" Bryce said.

She nodded. "Went out earlier, but he's inside now."

Bryce tugged my arm. "Follow me."

CHAPTER 43

☺ *Bryce* ☺

I had a better photo program on our computer at home, but this one would have to do. I clicked on the shot with the guy's face in the rocks. The resolution wasn't as good as our digital camera, but when I magnified it, you could see it was definitely a person and not just rocks.

"Whose hat does that look like?" I said.

Ashley leaned close. "Looks like the one Ricky wears."

I clicked on the search engine and typed in Ricky's name. Three Web sites came up that matched, but only one was about the Ricky we knew. It showed Ricky, bald and smiling, and told his sad story.

"Something about him bothers me," I said. "We saw him jogging. How many sick people run like that?"

She reminded me that our friend Jeff had gone on a long bike ride while dying of cancer.

"Yeah, but he struggled the whole way. Other than being bald and coughing, Ricky doesn't look sick. Have you seen him take any medicine? What if Ricky isn't really sick? What if he's pulling a fast one on the Lesters and . . ." I turned back to the computer, the ideas coming faster than I could speak.

"What?" Ashley said.

I clicked on the search engine and typed in the name of the hospital Sheila had mentioned. Information about the cancer ward came up. We scanned the name of the specialists. No Dr. Boyle.

"Web site could be old," Ashley said. "Or maybe he's moved on."

I went back to the search engine and typed in Griffin's name and the word *necklace*. Several stories popped up. One showed Griffin outside an expensive jewelry shop a week earlier, holding up a hand to block a camera. The caption read, "Tennis Ace Shopping Spree." The article listed the things Griffin had bought, including a gold necklace worth hundreds of thousands of dollars.

"He pretends to hate the paparazzi, yet he admits he buys the jewelry for more media attention."

"You think Ricky came here to steal that, Bryce? How would he know Griffin was going to be here?"

"The paparazzi knew he was here. Maybe Ricky knows someone who works with Griffin. Remember him asking us all about the inside of the boat?"

"You're right. He asked about Griffin's office."

"I don't know how he knew Griffin was here, but if he's conning the Lesters, they need to know."

CHAPTER 44

❀ Ashley ❀

I hated the thought of Ricky hurting Sheila. The way I looked at it, she was sacrificing a lot to marry this guy, helping him in what could be the last few months of his life. To think he might be faking it, that it was some ruse he had concocted to make money, made me really mad.

Still, something inside me wanted Ricky to be innocent. To really be sick, if you can believe that.

"If Ricky took the necklace, why would he stick around here?" I said.

Bryce sighed and shook his head. "Maybe he thinks he's so good no one will ever catch him. He must think he can fool anyone."

"Let's talk with Sheila."

Mom was wrestling Dylan into bed when we jumped onto the beach. We found Sheila sitting alone on a little knoll, a sad sight.

"Ricky's not feeling well tonight," she said, staring at the stars and sipping a bottle of Coke. She smiled. "Your mama get that little guy to bed yet?"

"He's putting up a fight," I said. "I don't know why. He never wins."

She chuckled. "Ricky and I have talked about having kids. He says it's best to wait and see what happens to him, but I'm not sure."

Bryce gave me a look like he wanted to choke Ricky. We watched the twinkling lights with Sheila. It should have been peaceful, but my stomach roiled.

"You said Ricky went out this morning," Bryce said. "What time?"

"Maybe 10. Why?"

"Just wondering," Bryce said. "I wish he could have come with us on our hike."

"He would have liked that."

"Sheila," I said, "did you guys know Griffin and Skylar were going to be out here?"

She shook her head. "First I heard about it was when you guys told us."

Bryce put his hands behind his head and leaned back. "Guess it's hard going with Ricky to the hospital all the time. That must get really tiring."

"Ricky's been so thoughtful about that," she said. "He only lets us drop him off. Says he doesn't want us watching what he has to go through."

I'll bet he doesn't.

Every answer, every piece of information made me feel sick about Ricky. Bryce and I had been wrong about people before, but this seemed like a slam dunk.

"You guys still staying the whole week?" Bryce asked.

"Far as I know," Sheila said.

The door opened on the deck of the Lesters' boat, and Ricky stepped out. Sheila waved as he trudged through the sand to us. I noticed a funny smell, something I couldn't place.

Ricky held out a hand and helped Sheila to her feet. "Hon, I'm not feeling well."

"What's wrong?" she said, feeling his forehead.

"Maybe this wasn't such a good idea. My stomach, my head. I'm achy all over. You think your mom and dad will mind us cutting out a little early?"

Bryce flashed me one of those we'd-better-do-something-fast looks.

"Sure, honey," Sheila said. "We can leave tonight if you want."

CHAPTER 45

☻ *Bryce* ☻

"Ash," I whispered, "radio the police from Griffin's boat. And have Mom get some dessert ready."

"Dessert?"

"I'll explain later. Hurry."

Sheila helped Ricky trudge slowly through the sand to her parents, and it was obvious Ricky was pleading his case to leave. I slipped around the back of their boat. A wet suit and goggles hung on the back railing.

As I came around front, Mr. Lester was saying, "Of course. We'll all go. Your health is the most important thing. No reason we can't get going right now."

"Believe me, I've had a good time," Ricky said. "It's been great."

Ricky seemed to stagger to the boat, and Sheila and the Lesters began carrying chairs and cooking equipment inside. When Mr. Lester came out for the anchors, I knew I had to do something.

"Hey, we were wondering if you'd have dessert with us," I said, jumping onto their deck. "Kind of a going-away type of thing."

"That's nice of you, son," Mr. Lester said. "Let me check with Ricky."

Ricky came out. "Thanks, man, but we really have to go."

When Mrs. Lester appeared, I said, "Mom's gone to a lot of trouble, and it'll just take a few minutes. We're going to miss you guys."

She looked at Ricky, who looked down and shook his head. "I'm not one to pass up food, Bryce," she said, "but I'm afraid we ought to be moving on."

"If you guys leave without saying good-bye to Dylan, he'll cry for three weeks."

"Oh, all right," Mr. Lester said. "A few more minutes shouldn't make much difference."

Ricky frowned and stiffened, but again Sheila held him up as he seemed to struggle through the sand to our boat.

I hurried to Mom and whispered, "Dylan still awake?"

"Of course. He'll fight Mr. Sandman till he's pinned to the pillow."

"Trust me."

"What?"

"Please."

It took two seconds for Dylan to bound out of bed when I clapped and held out my hands. He looked wide-eyed at Mom, no doubt wondering how he was getting away with this. As soon as he saw Mr. Lester, he squealed, "Grandpa!" and everybody laughed. Well, Ricky only smiled. He was really looking antsy.

Mom quickly dished up ice cream, giving me a curious smile. I was going to have some 'splainin' to do.

"So you're not feeling well, Ricky?" I said. "What is it? Headaches? Fever?"

"It's probably nothing," Ricky said. "This just takes a toll on you, you know? I might have gotten too much sun. So if you folks will—"

"Well, Bryce found your Web site earlier," Ashley said. "We were thinking we might contribute when we got back home. Maybe get some of the kids in our school to have a bake sale."

"Isn't that sweet?" Sheila said. "The Lord sure sent us good neighbors here."

"That's the truth," Mrs. Lester said.

Ricky smiled and nodded with his lips tight and slowly ate his ice cream. I noticed something white on the back of his head, just under his baseball cap.

Shaving cream. That's what Ashley must have smelled earlier! Ricky isn't bald. He shaves his head!

Ricky sat back and sighed. "You folks have been so good to us, but we really need to be—"

"I almost forgot," I said, grabbing a DVD from my suitcase. "I wanted to show you something. It won't take long."

"Bryce" Ashley said, as if I'd stepped over some line.

I skipped the intro and found Ashley's third-grade dance recital. She was in an orange outfit that made her look like a starved pumpkin. She dug her fingernails into my arm. "Why don't we show them the ballgame where you struck out five times?"

"Here it is," I said, flicking the clicker. "Our house back in Red Rock."

The DVD showed the house, the barn, and the red rocks in the distance.

"Ashleymobile!" Dylan shouted.

"That's my ATV," Ashley said.

"Oh, look at the dogs," Sheila said. "They're so cute."

Ashley told her everything she could think of about Pippin and Frodo: height, weight, eye color, that they were both on heartworm medication, the works.

Ricky finished his ice cream and stood, shifting from one foot to the other.

A swirling blue and red light flashed off the rocks behind us as a boat entered the channel.

Ricky peered out the window. "I really need to go. Sorry."

Ashley and I moved toward the door, blocking his way. Ricky just stared at us.

"The truth is, Mr. and Mrs. Lester," Ashley said, "we don't think Ricky is really sick."

CHAPTER 46

❀ Ashley ❀

My voice shook. In fact just about every muscle in my body shook. It's one thing to suspect someone, but it's a lot different to accuse him to his face, especially in front of people.

"Not sick?" Mrs. Lester cried. "What are you saying?"

"The lad has cancer!" Mr. Lester thundered.

Sheila moved to Ricky's side and reached for him, but he wrenched away. Mom grabbed Dylan and rushed him to his bedroom.

"What is this?" Ricky said, his gaze darting between Bryce and me. "What are you accusing me of?"

"Stealing Griffin's necklace for one," Bryce said. "And making these people think you're sick when you're just faking it to raise money."

"What?" Sheila said.

"This is preposterous," Mr. Lester said. "Did you invite us over here under false pretenses?"

Ricky closed his eyes and grabbed his forehead. "I'm going to be sick. Where's your bathroom?"

I pointed down the hallway.

Ricky ran inside, closed the door, and locked it. We heard him gagging, and it wasn't pretty. Suddenly I felt bad, like maybe we'd made a mistake, but when Bryce quickly whispered all our clues to the Lesters, their eyes widened and Sheila turned pale.

"You really think Ricky took that jewelry?" Sheila said.

Bryce nodded. "I saw his scuba suit. He must've stayed underwater until he got to the other side of Griffin's boat, climbed in, and gone to the office. Toomer might be able to describe how big he was and stuff."

The police boat pulled alongside ours, and Bryce went outside.

I put an arm around Sheila's shoulder. "I'm really sorry. I hope you aren't mad at us."

She took a breath. "I can't believe it. But if it's true, I'm glad I found out now."

The officer came aboard, and Bryce motioned to the bathroom. When Ricky didn't answer the officer's knock, I had the sinking feeling he'd crawled out the window. But then the door opened and he stepped out.

"Let's talk outside, son," the officer said.

When they passed the Lesters, Ricky muttered, "These kids are lying."

CHAPTER 47

☺ *Bryce* ☺

Ricky sat on the beach, a hand against his temple as if his head were going to explode. When the officer held up the diving suit, Ricky said, "It's not a crime to wear one of those."

"True," the officer said. "But it's a bit of a coincidence that you're this close to a crime scene in a place people never dive. And if the little girl got a look at your face—"

"I didn't take the necklace!" Ricky shouted. "Search me, for crying out loud. Search my room in the boat."

"You're giving me permission? I don't need a warrant?"

"Of course! Please!"

Easy, big boy, I wanted to say. *You're sick, remember?*

A crowd gathered along the shore. One of the most peaceful places on earth was now a hotbed of activity. People whispered and pointed. After searching the Lesters' boat, the officer cuffed Ricky and took him away. People moseyed back to their boats, and the Lesters were left behind, arms around each other and their daughter.

Ricky stared expressionlessly at them through the window, then glared at Ashley and me with such anger I could feel it.

CHAPTER 48

✖ Ashley ✖

We had a hard time getting Dylan to sleep because he couldn't find the little backpack he carried around. He called it his Huggy Bear. Bryce found it beside the toilet, and all was right with the world.

Sam called us together and said he and Mom had decided our time at Lake Powell was over. "Any objections to getting out of here in the morning? We can spend an extra day at the canyon before our hike."

"No," Bryce said, and I agreed.

"But," Sam added, "I've got something I want to do before we leave."

I figured Bryce was going fishing one more time, but he surprised me the next morning by asking if I'd go with him. We got in the little boat and headed into the channel. When we got far enough, we could see Griffin's boat in the distance, ringed by several smaller ones—the paparazzi and more security.

Bryce went straight for Adrian's boat. The curly-haired man was looking through binoculars as we pulled alongside.

"Get me any good shots?" he said.

"Sort of," Bryce said. "Unfortunately, I can't give your camera back." He explained what had happened on our hike with Griffin and that the police now had the camera as evidence.

Adrian sat up. "Evidence? Is it true somebody pilfered his chain? We've been wondering what was going on all night."

Others came out on deck and talked about the theft rumors and what they were going to do. They'd taken shots of the police boat, and one said he'd gotten a photo of a guy in handcuffs.

I noticed a wet suit hanging inside and asked what it was for.

"In case we need underwater shots," Adrian said. "Why?"

CHAPTER 49

☻ *Bryce* ☻

Ashley said we were leaving too soon—that Adrian or one of his cohorts could have stolen the necklace. I assured her Ricky was the guy.

"If the tabloids show pictures from inside Griffin's boat," I said, "that'll prove a photographer was in there, and we'll know I'm wrong."

Frankly, Ashley made a lot of sense, and I was starting to doubt myself.

We wanted to say good-bye to the Lesters before we pulled out that morning, but they had left during the night. I figured they probably went to see Ricky.

We passed Moby Houseboat and slowed, trying to get one more glimpse of our new friends. Only Terrance was on deck, and he didn't wave.

I figured we'd go back to the marina where we'd gotten the boat, but Sam pulled into a narrow canyon and slowed to a crawl. The wind off the water felt cooler, and fish swam below us.

Sam anchored at a strip of sand about 10 yards long. The place was deserted.

"Why are we stopping?" I said.

Sam glanced at Mom. "One more hike before we leave."

They had something up their sleeves and probably in their pockets too. Mom patted me on the back, a sure sign something was coming. She put a small shovel in my hand and pushed Ashley and me toward the sand.

Dylan cried, thinking we were leaving him. But Sam put him on his shoulders, and he and Mom followed us up a narrow trail to a rock ledge.

"Hope this isn't another corkscrew," Ashley said.

In a few minutes we were overlooking the canyon. The boat below looked like one of the pictures from the DVD we had seen about Lake Powell.

Sam led us to a red rock, then veered left to a grove of trees. The ground changed, looking green and lush instead of like a desert. He ducked under the branches and went straight toward a stream. It looked like he was counting his steps as he wound his way toward another rock.

Then he stopped. "Should be right here."

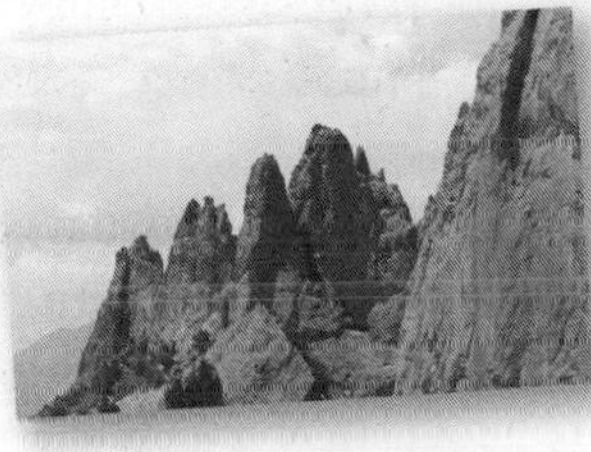

CHAPTER 50

❀ Ashley ❀

I'd been trying to figure out where we were going ever since Sam said we had to make one more stop. But when he pointed to a spot and told Bryce to dig, I was really mystified.

We were miles from anyone. The trees provided shade, and Mom and Dylan sat and watched. I hovered over Bryce's shoulder, trying to see.

Sam knelt, his knees cracking. "This is why Leigh was upset before we left."

"She wanted to dig something up?" I said.

Bryce's shovel struck something metal, and he looked at me like he had found gold.

Mom and Dylan came closer as Sam brushed dirt away. "It's still here," he said, smiling. "I was afraid the water might have washed it away."

Sam pulled a tree root out of the way and grabbed a metal box about the size of the money box Bryce and I use for our lemonade stand.

Sam placed it on the ground and flicked the latch. "You asked if I'd been here before, if I knew the trails and canyons and the fishing spot. The answer is yes."

Inside the box was a clear plastic bag containing pages and pictures. Mom gasped and put a hand over her mouth. "It really is here."

Sam pulled out the pictures. The first were black and white. A skinny kid held a string of fish. The next was the same kid with an older man and woman, standing by a marina and a small boat. The older man looked a lot like Sam.

"My parents brought me here when I was a kid. This is our time capsule. My dad's idea. He said we should keep a record of our lives, how we looked, what we were doing, our hopes and dreams."

Sam pulled out a scrawled page that read:

I want to fly fighter jets and go into space. I want to walk on Mars. I want to see foreign countries and fight bad guys.

Signed,
  Marshall Faulkner

A few months earlier Sam had told us that was his real name and why he had to change it after the terrorist attack.

It's hard to imagine adults as kids. You know they had to go to school, have vacations, and then grow up, but something keeps you from seeing them that way.

Sam handed us another picture. I could tell it was him, without the mustache, with a woman and a little baby. "That's Leigh, just a few months after she was born. We came here to get away, and I added this picture to the box. Then we came back again when Leigh was eight or nine."

He opened another piece of lined paper. "You have to promise you won't make fun of this."

Even though it had been written so many years ago, I could tell Leigh's handwriting. The note read:

> *I want to grow up and get married, have four children, live on a farm, and become a famous painter and a movie star.*

"That will be hard not to make fun of," Bryce said.

Sam gave him a look.

"But we won't, right, Ash?"

CHAPTER 51

☺ *Bryce* ☺

Sam showed us a letter his first wife had written before they were married, but he wouldn't let us read it. He showed some medals he had received while he was in the military, as well as some his father had won.

When we'd gone through all the stuff, Mom wiped away a tear and pulled something out of her pocket.

Sam took the pictures of us—him with Dylan on his shoulders back in Red Rock, Ashley and me playing tennis, a family photo complete with Pippin and Frodo. "When you get older and have families of your own," he said, "come back and add to the time capsule."

Mom pulled out a pad of paper and ripped off a couple of pages.

She handed Bryce and me pens and asked if we wanted to write what we wanted to do when we grew up, our hopes and dreams.

"You won't look at them, right?" I said.

"We'll just put them in there and maybe look at them a few years down the road," Sam said.

Ashley took a walk toward the stream, looking for a place to sit and write. Mom tried to show Dylan how to skip rocks, but every one he threw plunked.

I'm not much for writing. It doesn't come naturally like it does for Ashley, and sometimes it's hard to think of what I want to say. But still I tried.

> *I want to do good in school and maybe go to the Air Force Academy. I've thought about becoming a lawyer that defends innocent people. Or maybe a prosecutor who catches bad guys and puts them in jail.*

I looked at what I'd written and figured Ashley had already written a poem that rhymed perfectly. I was about to fold the page and stuff it in the plastic bag when I thought of something else. At first I was scared, afraid the wrong people might see it. But it was what was on my mind, so I figured it was okay.

> *More than anything I want Sam and Leigh to know God and believe in him. I want to be a better brother and son so they'll know what I believe is real. And I want Dylan to know God too.*

> *Signed,*
>   *Bryce Timberline, Esquire*

That's what lawyers put after their names, so why not? I wondered if Sam or Leigh would ever see it. Would we really come back here someday? What if we all died and no one ever knew about this spot? What if we became famous and the tabloids found our time capsule? That made me smile.

Ashley wandered back, and we stuffed our papers into the bag. Sam locked the box, and Dylan had fun covering it with dirt.

"What did you write?" I asked Ashley as we made our way back to the boat. "A sonnet?"

She rolled her eyes. "You think I'd tell you?"

"I'll bet you wrote that by the time you come back, you hope you won't have to take that seizure medicine anymore."

The way she smirked told me I was right.

"I didn't write just about me," she said.

I stopped her and let Sam get a little farther away. "I put something in there about Sam and Leigh. You think they'll see that and get mad?"

She smiled. "They'll have to get mad at both of us."

PART 3

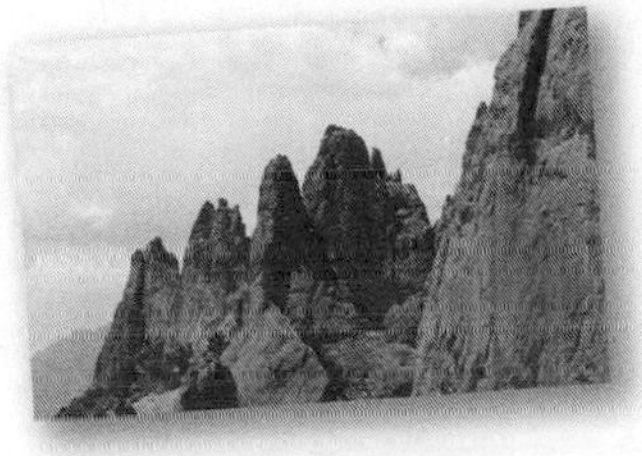

CHAPTER 52

Ashley

Katharine Lee Bates was inspired to write about the "amber waves of grain" and "purple mountain majesties" from Pikes Peak. I wonder what she would have written from the south rim of the Grand Canyon. The view at dawn took my breath and held it behind my back for a whole minute. You could tell people who had just driven up from the ones who had been there awhile. The newcomers still had their mouths open like they were looking at God, while the people who had been there awhile still had their mouths open but also had their cameras out.

You don't drive up to the Grand Canyon like you do to a Chuck E. Cheese's or an amusement park. The Grand Canyon covers more than a million acres, so you see different rock formations as you drive and catch glimpses of the river here and there. But once you're at the observation-deck railing, you feel like you're on top of the world.

The sun coming over the horizon cast a golden glow on the canyon, along with pinks and reds. It looked like a 3-D painting you could step into.

I heard several different languages and saw people from Asia, Europe, and Africa. It was a true global experience.

Bryce and I didn't have to carry Dylan, but we had to lug our share of water and camping equipment, which was just as heavy. We had figured how much water we'd need on a hot August day. And we brought elk jerky (which sounds worse than it is) and freeze-dried food from a specialty store. Finally we headed down the trail.

We had stayed two nights in a hotel near the village. It was nice to have a hot shower without worrying you'd drain the tank or run the generator too long, but I missed the lake. Bryce watched SportsCenter, and they had a short feature about Griffin and what a jewelry hound he was but nothing about the theft.

Mom's next book is a historical romance about a family leaving the "easy" life in the Midwest and traveling west in the early 1900s. She's written three books in the series—one on the Oregon Trail, another based on the Colorado gold rush, and one set during the Civil War.

"This one is about a guy running from the law who becomes a tour guide on the Colorado River," Mom said. "He meets a widow with her two children and has to choose between love and remaining free."

Mom doesn't usually talk about her books until they're finished, so I was surprised. "Where does God come in?"

She smiled. "Guess you'll have to read it."

CHAPTER 53

☺ *Bryce* ☺

I brought up the rear as we headed into the canyon with our walking sticks, watching Dylan's legs flop behind Sam in his carrier contraption. It would have been really funny if my blister didn't hurt so much.

I'd spent the last two days rubbing lotion on it, soaking it in the pool and the hot tub, and doing everything anybody said would help it heal faster. But as soon as we started down the trail, my shoes burned my feet.

We'd been walking a couple of hours when we stopped at a wide spot in the trail. Everybody drank water, and I slipped off my right shoe. When I saw blood on my white sock, I groaned and shoved the shoe back on. I didn't want anybody making a big to-do over a blister.

I tried to make myself laugh through the pain, like my friend Jeff. On our bike hike he had made up silly jokes and puns, and it actually worked. I smiled when I thought of Ashley with my problem. I'd have a sister with a blister. My sister's blister. We could play Twister with my sister's blister, mister.

"What are you laughing at?" Sam said.

I used one of his lines. "If I told you I'd have to kill you."

A few minutes later we stopped to let people walking up from the bottom pass us. They looked like they'd just been through a house of a hundred horrors. Their clothes were dusty, their faces hollow, and when we told them how far it was to the top, I thought they would faint.

We were on the Bright Angel Trail, clearly one of the most popular for mules. I could tell because there was mule poo and pee everywhere. The smell was awful, and I wished Mom would write a contemporary story about a widow who takes her kids in a helicopter over the canyon instead of hiking and camping. And then takes them to Disneyland instead of Six Blisters over Arizona.

By 10 a.m. it was nearly impossible to keep walking, but I had to. We stopped every few minutes to drink water. *At this rate we're going to run out before we even get to the bottom.*

I tried to think cool thoughts—air conditioners, blocks of ice, breezes, and pine trees with snow on their branches. But in my mind the air conditioners quit, the ice melted, the breezes turned blazing hot, and the pine trees caught fire. I even tried to think of penguins at the North Pole on a glacier, but the penguins got sunburned.

When your mind starts doing stuff like that, you know you're in trouble.

Dylan complained, even though he had a hat with an umbrella on it that kept his face in the shade. He had so much sunscreen on that he looked like he had jumped into a Coppertone vat.

With him crying, Sam struggling under the weight, and Ashley and me walking like pack mules, we made our way into the bowels of the canyon, the belly of the beast.

CHAPTER 54

✖ Ashley ✖

We had watched a couple of videos about the canyon in the hotel and found out that the guy they named Lake Powell after was the first to explore it—other than the Navajo and other Native Americans, of course. Some Indians had warned Powell that he shouldn't go into the canyon, that the gods would be upset with him. In fact, the first explorers who looked at the Colorado River from the south rim thought it was a six-foot-wide creek. Instead, it's 300 feet across in some places and as wild as they come.

Powell found out how wild when he took some boats down the

river and most of them were smashed. You can still take a rafting trip, and I think Mom wanted to, but with Dylan along it wasn't possible.

The heat became nearly unbearable, but there was nothing we could do but keep drinking water and walking. My tongue stuck to the roof of my mouth, and Mom yelled at me to stop when I poured a little water over my hat and let it roll onto my shoulders.

"Don't waste the water!" she said.

She doesn't usually yell—I think the last time was when I tried to boil an egg in the microwave. She'd flown across the kitchen and pushed the Stop button before the thing exploded.

There wasn't much wildlife to look at, like in the videos. Those showed deer, cougars, coyotes, and little scurrying animals, but that was at the bottom of the canyon. On the trail it was too hot for any-thing but lizards, and even they stayed in the shade. But the canyon left me in awe every time I looked out. I'd take a few steps, my feet crunching the dirt and tiny rocks, then look at the scenery, then take another step. It was like standing next to God's bay window, open to the whole world.

The sunrise had been dramatic, like someone had pulled back a curtain on creation. Now that curtain had revealed an oven.

"You sure people actually camp here in August?" I said.

The river was a brown snake when we started, and I could see why Powell thought it was small.

"Why couldn't you write a book in Hawaii?" I said.

"Hard to pull a wagon all the way there, Ash," Bryce said.

We came to a sheer cliff, and I hugged the rock wall, inching down. Small rocks crackled and fell. I thought I saw someone dart out of sight behind us.

CHAPTER 55

☉ *Bryce* ☉

There comes a point when you know you should just turn around and find a hotel, and I reached that point before anyone else. It was partly because of my blister and partly because Mom started telling weird stories about accidents in the canyon. Part of me wanted to plug my ears and go, "Na na na na." Another part of me was really interested.

Most people get in trouble here because they don't bring enough water. Some get so hot and dehydrated that they get heatstroke, which is basically your body overheating and shutting down. Mom said one dead guy was found with two full water bottles. She told another tale of four men who got lost in the labyrinth of canyons and sealed a note in a tin can giving their names and where they were from.

"They never found their bodies," Mom said, with that storyteller glint in her eye. "Maybe we'll come upon their bones."

"Yeah, we can give them some elk jerky," I said.

"It happened to James Higgins when he reversed this route," Mom continued. "Nineteen years old. Parked his motorcycle and hiked the Hermit Trail. His itinerary said he would hike the Tonto Trail down to Bright Angel, go to the Colorado, then come back up. Four days. And even though it was early July, he was from Nevada, which is pretty hot."

"So he should have known what heat can do," I said.

Mom nodded. "When he didn't show up on the south rim, searchers went out. Didn't find anything the first day. The second day, on the Tonto Trail, east toward Horn Creek Canyon—" she pointed—"the searchers found motorcycle tools. Then boots. Then jeans. Then a soap dish with his driver's license and library card. When they found him, he was in his underwear and dehydrated. He was hyperthermic."

"Isn't that where you get too cold?" Ashley said.

"No, that's hyp-*o*-thermic, the opposite. Hyp-*er*-thermic is just a fancy word to describe heatstroke. If your body temperature goes up and stays up, you die. It cooks your brain, which is why people do weird things. And it can happen quickly. If you stop sweating, your body temperature goes up. Things shut down. You can have a seizure. People look drunk, wobbling as they walk."

"I need to sit," Ashley said.

"What happened to the biker guy?" I said.

"The hikers who found him got a ranger to dispatch a helicopter. Higgins died on the flight to the clinic—only five minutes away."

CHAPTER 56

✖ Ashley ✖

I didn't want to hear about seizures. I just wanted to get to the
camp and wait for the sun to go down—or better still, turn around.

"Why do you have to hike here, Mom?" I said. "Can't you go on
the Internet?"

"It's not the same," she said. "I want to walk where my characters walk. Experience what they see, smell, hear, feel."

"I don't think anybody would want to smell what I smell,"
Bryce said.

More hikers passed us from below.

"Hi," Dylan said.

The people smiled and nodded, but they looked too exhausted to lift a hand. Most of them carried hiking canes like us.

I didn't feel hungry, but Mom made us stop and eat pretzels, crackers, and trail mix. She kept saying we needed fuel, and she seemed especially concerned about Sam. "Your color's too dark," she said.

"You've been reading too many Web sites," he said.

I noticed something weird. None of us had sweat stains, not even Sam. It was so hot that any moisture on your skin immediately evaporated.

A man and his wife passed from behind and offered weak smiles. We would pass them later. Then they would pass us again as we took pictures or stopped for a drink. Mom finally spoke with them and discovered they were from Germany, spoke very little English, but thought Americans were loud and dirty.

I wanted to tell them it was the donkeys, not the Americans, making all the mess.

CHAPTER 57

☺ *Bryce* ☺

We'd been hiking for hours when Sam reminded Mom not to walk on her toes, that she needed to step heel first.

"Now you're going to tell me how to walk?" she said, turning on him.

Sam shrugged, but I could tell she had hurt his feelings.

We made it to a rock above the inner gorge. My feet felt like they were about to fall off. I've played a lot of basketball and had grueling games and practices, but coming down that hill was the hardest thing I've done. I couldn't imagine hiking all the way back up.

We finally made it to the Bright Angel Campground and collapsed.

Cottonwood trees surrounded the camp. Sam looked happy to get Dylan off his back, and Dylan was equally happy to run around and stretch his legs.

I was never so glad to find a bathroom in my life, and Mom and Ashley seemed just as excited and relieved, no pun intended.

I could have filled our water bottles from a faucet, but I wanted to try out our purifier. Ashley led the way to Bright Angel Creek, and I pumped enough for all our water bottles. Ashley kicked off her shoes and socks and found she had the beginnings of a couple of good blisters too. When her feet hit the water I could almost hear her skin hiss. The creek was only a few inches deep, but we had fun throwing water on each other. My legs ached, and my blister was even worse.

When I was done pumping water, I sat on a rock in the middle, my feet dangling in the stream, and looked out at the camp. There was room for fewer than a hundred people, and it was already almost half full.

I wondered if there were fish in any part of the creek and wished I'd brought a pole and lures. Movement in the trees startled me, and several pairs of brown eyes stared back. It turned out to be deer, and all the splashing and laughing didn't seem to bother them.

That wasn't the case for our German friends. They looked at us like we had broken some billion-year-old peace treaty. The man said something in German, motioned toward our backpacks, and walked away shaking his head. I hoped they'd find a different trail.

When we returned to our stuff I saw what the fuss was about. Our backpacks lay open, and a bunch of food wrappers flitted in the breeze.

"Who did this?" Mom said.

I pointed to a log nearby. "Check out our little four-legged friend."

A rock squirrel perched on the log with his cheeks full of one of

Sam's PowerBars. I was about to gather up the trash when Ashley caught my arm. "Hang on."

The squirrel finished his PowerBar and hopped to Sam's back- pack, which lay unopened. He flipped the zipper a couple of times with his front paws, then grabbed it with his teeth and pulled. He pried it open and yanked out a bag of trail mix. He couldn't figure out the Ziploc, so he just tore it with his teeth, and the raisins, nuts, and candy spilled. Mom took a picture of him, and Ashley named him Chuck after a guy in our school who spends a little too much time at the lunch table, if you know what I mean.

We set up our tents and rested before dinner. It felt good to be out of the sun, but inside the tent was like a toaster, so I wandered back to the creek.

It was so different looking up at the top of the canyon rather than down. It looked a little like places we had seen at Lake Powell, but even more dramatic. The rock formations soared. Some looked like God had stacked boulders on top of each other that were going to tumble down the incline. Others rose smoothly, and you could see many different layers.

Some people think a place like the Grand Canyon makes you think about God, but I'm not sure. I overheard some people talking about the billions of years it took to make the canyon. It told me that if you believe in God and that he created the world, it leaves you in awe of what he's done. Otherwise, you can somehow be in awe of evolution and decide that we're just specks of dust on a spinning planet. You may be in awe of Mother Nature, whatever that is, and you appreciate the beauty of the rocks and trees and birds and flow- ers, but in the end you're just part of the great nonplan.

I wasn't a Christian when Dylan was born, but I took one look at him and knew God was real. You can't view a baby's perfect fingers,

toes, eyes, nose, mouth, and think that that intricate design happened by chance.

Even if he does get on my nerves.

CHAPTER 58

✿ Ashley ✿

I wanted to be alone when the sun went down, so after dinner I
got my diary and hiked away from camp. Clouds rolled in and thunder rumbled in the distance, making it a little cooler than when
we'd hiked down.

I hadn't planned on liking this trip, but the scenery and being
with my family gave me a feeling I hadn't had in a while. I was sad
Leigh wasn't here to share it, especially after seeing the pictures of
her as a little girl.

I closed my eyes, put my feet in the stream, and listened to the gurgling and lapping. A raven cawed above me, and laughter echoed off the rock wall behind me.

I wrote:

> Time is a lot like this stream. It cuts through your life, day by day, leaving canyons of hurt or happiness. Some walls of wounds never heal. For others, time produces a faith that can't be shaken, smooth rocks of belief.

It was sounding kind of cheesy, so I stopped, but I knew I was on to something. Sometimes life *is* like a stream that flows gently and feels cool to your feet. Other times it rages like the Colorado River and cuts deep. Our dad dying was a raging river, and it probably cut scars in us that will always be there. But those bad times make you appreciate the good all the more and teach you that you can get through the rapids. And when you come out the other side you're that much more grateful to be alive.

Just as slowly as the morning curtain had revealed all the colors and splendors of the canyon, the evening shadows descended and pulled a blanket over the world. A line of darkness began behind me, then crept along the streambed, across the river, and up the side of the sheer rock wall in the distance. The walls went from brown to orange to red, the reverse of what we had seen early in the day.

You can measure your life by shadows, I think. Shadows that overwhelm and turn the world dark. Shadows that sneak up on you.

> It's all about the shadows. How we handle them. We can let them cover us, or we can choose to build a fire or pick up a flashlight and shine a light in the darkness.

Something moved on the bank, and tiny rocks skittered into the water.

I turned, expecting a deer or maybe a lizard.

When I didn't see anything, I remembered a cougar from the video. Was something watching me? Someone? Maybe the German lady wanted to make sure I wasn't littering.

CHAPTER 59

⊙ *Bryce* ⊙

When the sun went down, a slight breeze that felt like heaven blew through the canyon. We milled around the camp and got to know a few people and where they were from. Ashley tried to ignore a guy from Canada.

"You call your country a melting pot," he told her. "We like to think ours is a tossed salad."

She smiled but glanced back up the canyon. I pulled her away and asked her what was wrong.

"I just get the feeling we're being watched."

I pointed to the log where the same rock squirrel sat. "Ever since he got a taste of the good life, he's been watching us for another chance at dessert."

"I'm serious," Ashley said. "And it's more than a feeling. I've caught sight of someone a couple of times."

"Maybe a secret admirer. That guy from Canada?"

She rolled her eyes. "Why do you think I like every cute guy that comes along?"

"Cute? So you admit you think he is?"

She socked me on the shoulder.

We sat and I leaned back to gaze at the sky. It was one thing looking at stars from the boat on Lake Powell, but quite another looking at them framed by rocks that loomed like monsters. A coyote howled in the distance, and another across the river picked up the song.

"The stars sure make you feel small," Ashley said.

"They make me tired," I said.

The guy from Canada brought out—no joke—a ukulele and started playing "Somewhere Over the Rainbow." Everyone joined in but Ashley and me. The guy wasn't bad, but ukuleles aren't my thing.

I barely remember collapsing in the tent with Sam and Dylan. The little guy insisted on a story, but Sam fell asleep while making one up. That made Dylan giggle until he dozed too. I drifted off with a smile.

CHAPTER 60

❀ Ashley ❀

As Mom and I lay trying to sleep I had to ask how she felt about Sam's time capsule.

"It sure gave me a new insight into him and Leigh," she said.

"You still glad you married him?"

She rolled up on one elbow and looked at me in the darkness. "Of course. I love him. You mean because he's not a Christian yet? I can't waste time worrying about what might have been or could have been. I wasn't a believer when we found each other. If I met him today and he wasn't a Christian, I wouldn't even date him, but I'd try like everything to get him to see the truth."

She put her hands behind her head and lay back down. "I'm trusting God is working on him and Leigh."

We fell silent for several minutes, but when I could tell from her breathing that Mom was still awake, I said, "What do you think I'll do when I grow up?"

She chuckled. "Sometimes I think you and Bryce will wind up on a police force somewhere." She reached out and touched my head. "You know how special I think you are. I think God has big plans for you, kiddo."

I love it when Mom calls me that. Maybe I'll get tired of it, and maybe I won't want her to use it in front of my friends. But the way she says it tells me she's somebody who sees me at my worst and still believes in me.

"Specifically," I said. "When I'm 25, where do you think I'll be?"

"Let's make it to 14 first," she said. When I didn't laugh, she turned to face me, and her inflatable mat squeaked. We both laughed—it sounded funny. "Ex-*cuse* me!" she said, and I laughed so hard I thought I was going to cry.

She took my hands in hers. "Let me turn the question around. Where do *you* want to be when you're 25?"

I shrugged. "I don't know. Maybe a writer. I like solving mysteries, so maybe I could go to detective school or something. Or a special ed teacher. Is it wrong to want to stay at home? Leaving kind of scares me, and then at other times I can't wait to get out of there."

"I had the same feeling when I was your age. For some kids it's good to get away as soon as they're 18. Others need more time. You'll know when the time comes."

A plane flew over, heading west, glinting in the moonlight. We played a game Mom and I had played since I was little. We'd see a bus, a train, a plane, or a car and ask the other, "Who's in there?" The answer can be funny. Sometimes sad.

"What if your future husband is on that plane?" she said. "I was married to your dad when I was 24, you know. That's only eleven years away for you."

"Ten and a couple of months," I said.

"Your future husband could be flying to California right now for a screen test."

"I'll marry a movie star?"

"You might. Or a ukulele player from Canada."

"Stop!" I said. "Bryce told you? He's going to pay for that."

She laughed, then yawned. "This is what I imagined for the characters in my story. The mom would talk to her daughter about life, give advice, and then be forced to eat her own words when she meets a man running from his past, God, and the law."

We lay there awhile just looking at the stars. I heard men talking in hushed voices about baseball. Sports is one thing you can't escape, even in the Grand Canyon.

"You think Dad sees us?" I whispered.

"Of course, and I know he's proud of you."

I rolled over on my mat. "Love you, Mom."

CHAPTER 01

◔ *Bryce* ◔

Something banged my shoulder, shaking me out of a deep sleep. Dylan's face was inches from mine, tears dripping from his nose.

"Go back to sleep," I whispered. I buried my face in my pillow.

"I can't. I'm scared."

"Nothing is going to get you, buddy. Now just go back—"

"But he's trying to get Huggy Bear," he said, sobbing. Huggy Bear is his little backpack with all the zippers.

I lifted my head and faced him. "You were having a bad dream. Nobody wants your Huggy Bear. Put your head down and it'll be morning before you know it."

Just as I drifted off, I heard his soft, rhythmic breathing and knew he was close. Suddenly he sat up. "No!"

"Dylan, be quiet," I said, worried he'd wake Sam.

He clutched his Huggy Bear to his chest and whispered, "He's trying to get it."

"Who is?"

"The man out there."

Something moved at the back of the tent. An animal? A hand?

I sat up. Faint light from the bathrooms silhouetted a hooded figure outside our tent.

"Sam!" I whispered.

Nothing.

The figure stood there, looking at us. I carefully unzipped my backpack, pulled out my flashlight, and turned it on. As soon as I did, the stranger ran away.

CHAPTER 62

✖ Ashley ✖

I heard the commotion and reached to wake Mom, but she was gone. It was still dark when I crawled out. The moon sat straight above us.

". . . thought he saw someone trying to get in our tent," Sam said. "He's a little shaken up."

Bryce walked up, scanning his flashlight back and forth on the ground.

Mom held Dylan close in the slightly cooler air. I insisted she stay with Dylan and Sam. "Bryce and I will take the other tent."

When Mom and Dylan were settled with Sam, Bryce found a fresh set of footprints. "He must have gone that way, toward the stream. You up for some investigating?"

I looked back. "It could have been someone in camp. What if he's still out there?"

"The better question is, why was he at our tent?"

"Maybe the squirrel told him about the PowerBars," I said, trying to hide my fear.

"I'm going. Stay if you want."

I followed him into the night, watching the flashlight beam carefully. There were footprints, but how could Bryce tell them apart? When we reached the stream, he knelt and studied a tennis-shoe print that looked fresh. "Here's more."

I looked at the impression in the sand and saw several smaller prints nearby. "Duh! That's your own footprint from earlier. And Dylan's is right beside it."

He sat on a rock and flicked the light off. Insects buzzed and clicked music of their own. Bryce tossed a pebble in the water, and the moon's reflection rippled.

"Maybe it was that German couple," I said. "Maybe they want us off the trail."

"Yeah, or it could have been the Canadian coming to serenade you."

"Maybe Dylan just had a bad dream," I said.

Bryce turned. "That's what I accused him of. But Dylan was right. I saw someone behind our tent. I hate it when grown-ups don't trust what I say. I did the same thing to Dylan."

We sat in silence a few minutes. I was about to suggest we try to get some sleep when I heard footsteps. Bryce put a finger to his lips.

A shadowy figure crept along a trail near the boulders. The man wore a hooded sweatshirt—weird because it was so hot.

"Let's follow him," Bryce whispered.

CHAPTER 63

☻ *Bryce* ☻

We stayed well back with our flashlight off and followed the hooded figure back to camp. "I think he's near the tents," I whispered.

We let our eyes adjust. Then I spotted the hood moving behind the last row of tents, near the one Sam and Mom were in.

"What if this guy knows who Sam is?" Ashley whispered.

"A terrorist in the Grand Canyon? Seems like a lot of trouble to go to when he could find Sam in Red Rock or at the airstrip. Probably just somebody who needs food or money."

"Then why is he targeting only our tent?"

We raced forward, keeping our heads down, then crouched and tried to control our breathing.

I aimed the flashlight and was about to turn it on when Ashley grabbed my arm. "Give me your light. There's something on my leg."

I put my hand over the end of the light and clicked it. I didn't see anything at first. Then I noticed something sticking out of the folds of Ashley's sweatpants. She stiffened, and I pulled up her sweats a little. A tail rose.

"Hold still, Ash. It's a scorpion."

CHAPTER 64

❋ Ashley ❋

I screamed, and Bryce knocked the scorpion off me with his flash-light. It scurried under our tent.

My scream woke up everyone, and when people came out I told them about the scorpion but not the person in the sweatshirt. Bryce went to investigate as Mom and Sam came out of their tent.

The Canadian guy came over and pulled up the tent mat. The scorpion was gone. "Good thing you weren't wearing sandals," he said. "Those things sting your feet, and someone would have to carry you out of here."

Bryce returned a few minutes later shaking his head. "Didn't find anybody."

"You saw the guy near our tent?" Sam said.

Bryce nodded. Dylan had slept through the whole episode, and Mom returned to keep an eye on him.

Sam sighed. "We still have a few hours before sunup. Let's make sure there are no critters inside your tent."

He helped us shake out our sleeping mats. Others in the camp were doing the same with theirs. Sam zipped us inside, and we tried to sleep.

I couldn't. I imagined tarantulas and scorpions waiting for us to step outside. I kept my shoes on because of what the Canadian guy said. If you've ever tried to sleep with your shoes on, you know your feet get hot and sweaty and you start concentrating on your feet instead of going to sleep.

Bryce was just as spooked, though not about arachnids and his feet. He turned his flashlight on every few minutes and pushed it through the back flap to scan the area behind us.

I stared at the stars through the mesh opening at the top. I was afraid that if I went to sleep I'd wake up to see a hooded face—or a huge scorpion—looking back at me.

"Our problems will be over tomorrow," I said.

"How do you figure?"

"We're going on the Tonto Trail. There won't be as many people."

"That doesn't mean we won't have a problem."

I stared at the stars until they got blurry and I couldn't keep my eyes open. Hot as it had been, I couldn't believe I wanted the sun to come up.

CHAPTER 65

☺ *Bryce* ☺

Sam woke us before daylight. Most campers had moved out by the time we left and were headed the way we had come, getting an early start before it got too hot. Mom seemed excited by the hike ahead, and Sam gave her a few minutes to take pictures and jot notes about what we'd seen.

"Maybe you can have a guy terrorize people at their campsite," I said. "But make sure he gets stung by a scorpion."

Watching the sunrise from deep inside the canyon gave it a more personal feel, like the golden glow was saying hello to us.

I wonder if there are canyons in heaven and whether my dad

explores them. I think of him at the strangest times. Sometimes I'll watch a TV show or just walk down the hall at school and start thinking about him and what might have been. I don't want people to feel sorry for me, so I don't talk about him a lot, but the thought of him is always there, like a pebble in your shoe on a long hike.

We got our hats and shirts wet in the stream, made sure our water jugs were filled, and then hit the trail. My blister felt better, but it wasn't long before I could feel it rubbing again. I tried to put that out of my mind.

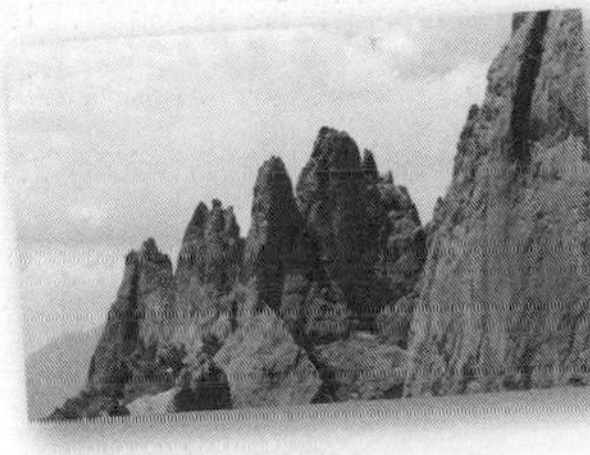

CHAPTER 66

❀ Ashley ❀

We'd been on the trail only about an hour when Bryce had to stop. His foot was killing him and mine hurt too, though I let him take the blame.

It hurt so much that it was hard to appreciate the view, but when I looked up, the trail got lost in a sea of multicolored rocks. The ridges and rock formations were impossible to count. At one point I looked back the way we had come and couldn't recognize it. Had we really been through that maze of stones and trees?

It was eerily quiet now, like we were alone in the canyon. The first day we had passed tons of people. Now there wasn't anyone, and I almost missed the mule doo.

A crow flew over—they call them ravens here, black as night with a sound right out of one of those scary movies. I thought of Edgar Allan Poe and his poem "The Raven," and it creeped me out. "Nevermore," said the bird, perched on some statue. This bird didn't have quite the same diction, but its voice pierced me just as bad as the guy in the poem.

We started out slowly again and made it to shade where we sat on rocks. People say camping is fun, but the rocks are still as hard as . . . well, rocks, and camping gear is heavy. My knees felt like Jell-O from all the lugging and climbing. Through a gully we could see a small section of the river. It didn't look that fast until a raft appeared and raced through. The people on it wore orange life vests. Suddenly, the raft hit rough water and the front went straight up. I thought everybody was going to fall out, but somehow they hung on and the raft crashed down and kept going.

We ate smashed peanut-butter-and-jelly sandwiches. Mom kept saying we needed fuel, so I ate a bag of pretzels and drank about a gallon of water.

"Where are we going to sleep tonight?" Dylan said.

Mom told him we were going to find a quiet place away from everyone else, and that made me glad. No reason to worry about the hooded stranger.

CHAPTER 67

☺ *Bryce* ☺

It felt like we were the only people on earth as we set up camp in the early afternoon. We might as well have been on the moon. We sat in the shade of our tents and watched chipmunks play on a rock, scampering back and forth from some nearby trees and an old log.

We had filled our water bottles at the last camp, and Mom said we'd get to the next water station the next day. I found Dylan making mud pies with a whole gallon of water. Mom was busy with dinner and hadn't paid attention. She didn't yell at him, but I could tell by her face that losing all that water scared her.

As the sun passed farther to the west, the shade from the mountain reached us, and it felt like the temperature went down about 10 degrees. I had thought I'd be bored during the hike, that I'd want to *do* something, but now I was so drained I just wanted to sit.

As we sat resting near the tents in the late afternoon we were startled when a woman walked by and stopped. "Mrs. Timberline?" she called out in a soft voice. "Is that you?"

Mom stood and brushed off her pants. "Sheila?"

CHAPTER 68

❀ Ashley ❀

It was a bizarre coincidence to run into Sheila on the back side of the Grand Canyon in what seemed like the most remote place in the world. But she didn't seem to think so. It was also strange that she was carrying one water bottle on the side of her backpack and wearing skimpy tennis shoes.

"I told Mom and Dad I was going to try to find you," she said. "They're at Phantom Ranch. Mom showed me the trail you'd be on."

"What happened to Ricky?" I said.

Something passed over her face, and she looked at the ground. "We went to see him at the jail. Turns out you were right. He was playing us like a fiddle. Lied to us about his disease. Took all the money from the Web site. He confessed he dragged us out to Lake

Powell because he heard that tennis guy with all the jewelry was going to be there. I thought it was weird that he rented the scuba stuff, but Ricky's always been flighty like that."

"Did they find the necklace?" Bryce said.

"Ricky said he threw it in the water. He's going to lead the police back there to find it."

"What's going to happen to him?" Mom said.

"Tell you the truth, I don't care. He deserves whatever they give him."

"And you?" she said.

She looked at the canyon walls. "I'm okay."

I didn't believe it. She had been planning to marry a guy who had lied to her and her parents.

"I know the Lord will look after me and my family," she said. "It's hard to know you were lied to by the person you were going to marry and that he hurt a lot of other people. But Dad says time heals all wounds. And I have the Lord."

"Where are you staying tonight?" I said.

"I'll probably head back to Phantom Ranch if I can find my way out of here." She looked around. "Sure are a lot of places to explore."

"Phantom Ranch is too far," Sam said, looking at the map. "You don't want to be hiking in the dark. You have a permit to camp down here?"

"Do I need one?" she said.

"Stay with us," Mom said.

"That's kind of you, but I'm sure my parents will be worried."

"Better that you get a good night's rest and head out in the morning than chance getting lost tonight," Mom said. "We'll make a map so you'll be sure to find it."

CHAPTER 69

☾ *Bryce* ☾

Mom laid out the food—almost all we had left—and we dug in. We'd been following her directions to eat a lot of salty, carb-loaded food to keep our energy up and drink lots of water. I was getting really tired of the freeze-dried stuff, but Sheila chowed down like she hadn't had a thing all day. Mom filled her water bottle and gave a cautious glance at our supply.

"You know, we might just go back with you to Phantom Ranch tomorrow morning," Mom said.

Sheila looked at her quickly, then smiled. "That would be great.

I didn't want to say anything, but I'm kind of nervous about finding it alone."

"What about the Hermit Trail?" Ashley said.

"We can adjust our plans a little," Mom said.

"I know my mom and dad will be happy to see you. They talked so much about you after the thing with Ricky. They went on and on about how nice you treated us and what a fine Christian family you are."

I had to wonder what Sam thought about that.

CHAPTER 70

✖ Ashley ✖

Sheila took a big interest in Dylan, playing with him after dinner and giggling with him in the tent. I guess it helped take her mind off her troubles.

Sam paced near the camp, watching for a ranger. He said they might kick Sheila out if they found out she wasn't approved for the campground, but no ranger came.

Dylan hopped out of the tent with his Huggy Bear on his back and announced he was going for a hike. Mom smiled and seemed to enjoy his having someone to play with.

"Don't go far," she said.

He and Sheila walked off, holding hands and laughing.

"Where is Sheila going to sleep?" Bryce said.

"Mom says Sam will stay outside tonight to give her room."

Bryce shook his head. "There's room in our tent if we scrunch up."

CHAPTER 71

☺ *Bryce* ☺

I went for Sam's backpack and mat and noticed Sheila's stuff in the corner. I don't usually snoop, but there was something odd about her backpack. It looked just like one I saw in a shop at the village. It was cheap, like a souvenir for a kid, but not something you'd take into the Grand Canyon.

I unzipped the top, just to take a peek, and what I saw made my knees buckle.

A blue sweatshirt with a hood.

CHAPTER 72

✖ Ashley ✖

I found Bryce in the tent and scolded him for looking through Sheila's backpack. When he pulled out the blue sweatshirt, I stared at it like it was a snake.

"Coincidence?" Bryce said. "Or was Sheila trying to get in our tent last night?"

A thousand thoughts whipped through my mind. "Dylan! She's out there with Dylan!"

Bryce stuffed the shirt back in, and we flew out of the tent.

"What's the hurry?" Mom said as we kicked up dust near her.

"Just going to look for Dylan," I said.

"He's with Sheila," Mom called after us, as if we didn't know.

Shadows covered the canyon, and as we came to the top of a knoll, Dylan and Sheila weren't in sight. My heart pounded like a steam engine.

Dylan's squeal echoed off some boulders ahead of us. We took off, me thinking the worst. Maybe Sheila hated us for exposing her fiancé. Maybe she was so out of her mind that she blamed us, and to punish us she was going to hurt the person we loved.

Bryce jumped up on a rock and stopped, leaning against another giant boulder. I joined him and looked at the rock-strewn path. Sheila and Dylan were hunched over, studying something on the ground.

Instead of crying, Dylan had a smile as wide as the canyon. "Look, we found some old foxholes!"

"Fossils," Sheila said. "Come see."

Bryce and I climbed down, and sure enough there were rocks with imprints of bugs on them. A huge rock had reptile footprints, as if God had preserved the travels of some little creature just for us. Sheila tried to pry a rock out of the ground.

Bryce told her to stop. "We're not supposed to disturb anything here."

"Who's going to notice one little rock in a million valleys full of them?" she said. "Well, you're right. We should leave this place like we found it. Probably took a million years to make that thing in the rock."

I had a queasy feeling all the way back to camp. Part of me wanted to confront Sheila right there and ask why she had tried to break into our tent. Another part wanted to think the best of her. Maybe someone else had a hooded sweatshirt—anyone could have bought one at the village. She seemed genuine in her faith in God. Still, something didn't seem right.

When we got back, Dylan bounded in and told Mom all about the "foxholes" he'd seen. We spent the last few minutes of the sunset looking at the different colors in the canyon. I wondered if I'd ever be able to describe it to my friends.

I asked Mom if I could help get Dylan ready for bed. "I'd never pass up an offer like that," she said.

Dylan dumped a pound of sand from each shoe, took off his socks and other clothes, then got ready for bed. We'd passed a lot of people who looked at us like we had three heads when they saw Dylan. I guess they thought somebody that little shouldn't be hiking, but he was doing better than all of us. He had no blisters, had quit complaining about the heat, and always seemed to have energy.

"Did you like your hike with Sheila?"

"Yeah. She's fun."

I helped him pull a shirt over his head. His little arms rose straight in the air and his ribs stuck through the baby fat on his tummy. "Were you scared of her?"

He scrunched his chin into a pout but didn't answer.

"You screamed out there before we got to you. What was that about?"

He leaned forward and put a finger to his lips. "It's a secret."

"Whose secret?"

"Me and Sheila's."

"You can tell me," I whispered.

He looked up as the tent flap opened. "What's going on with my little man in here?" Sheila said.

She unzipped her backpack and pulled out some lip balm. "I gave Dylan one of my extras, but it's our secret, right?" She tweaked his nose and he giggled.

Wind whistled through the canyon and sounded like a tank. Sam hung our remaining scraps of food in a tree and measured the rest of our water. The stars were out. It looked like they were trying to put on a show before the moon made its appearance.

I wanted to talk to Mom about Sheila and Dylan, but Sheila hung around. Since our tent was smaller, Sam suggested we switch and let Mom, Dylan, and Sheila sleep in ours.

I put my head down, waiting for Sam to get settled so I could talk, but my eyelids were so heavy I closed them for just a second.

This is a big mistake.

CHAPTER 73

☺ *Bryce* ☺

I woke first and checked my watch. It was 5:30, and Sam had said he wanted to get going by 6. I decided to let him and Ash sleep a little longer and went to the bathroom in the rocks. I glanced back and saw our other tent move.

I hurried back but didn't see anyone, yet some of our food was gone. Two liters of water were missing too. Two liters we couldn't spare.

Maybe Sam had moved them, but I couldn't find them. I knocked his foot, which was sticking out of our tent, and he came barreling out like some bear whose cub was in danger. That woke Ashley, of course. Sam shook his head and rubbed his eyes, then looked at his watch. He thought I was just telling him it was time to get up, but when I pointed out the water supply and the missing food, he went to the smaller tent and opened the flap.

"Sheila's gone," he said.

I looked inside. Mom sat up next to Dylan.

"Where do you think she went?" Mom said.

Sam shook his head.

Ashley picked up a piece of paper lying under a rock by the tent, unfolded it, and read it out loud.

"Dear Timberlines,

Thanks for letting me stay with you and for your kindness and hospitality. I'm going back to the hotel to my parents, and I hope you won't mind if I borrow some water. I didn't want to wake you. God bless you all."

"Should we go after her?" Ashley said.

"She can't be far," Sam said. "I'm of half a mind to just let her go."

"I thought she said her parents were staying at Phantom Ranch," I said.

Sam shrugged.

A wail pierced the darkness. We rushed the small tent and found Dylan throwing things around.

"I can't find my Huggy Bear!"

CHAPTER 74

✖ Ashley ✖

Mom has taught me to think the best of people, to take them at
their word, not to judge them by what they wear or what other people say about them. But Mom also writes fiction and knows characters can come out different in the end than when you first meet
them. I had that feeling about Sheila, and I was getting mad.

"I want my Huggy!" Dylan cried.

"Quicker we strike camp, the quicker we'll find him," Sam said.

Bryce gave me a knowing glance.

Then Sam turned to us. "You think you two could help your

mother get on the trail? I'd like to find this girl." He put on his backpack and pulled out his map. "My guess is she's headed toward Hermit Trail. I'll meet you a little farther with some water from the next stop." He took the GPS from around his neck and handed it to Bryce. "This will keep you on the right path."

Sam kissed Mom and ran toward the trail with his backpack. I wondered how far he'd get at that pace. Something inside felt weird watching him go, like we'd never see him again.

"Sam!" I yelled.

He stopped and turned.

I waved. "Be careful."

Sam gave me his patented smile, tipped his white hat, and continued.

Maybe I'm being oversensitive.

The good news was we didn't have much food to carry. The bad news was that the sun was just coming up, and it was already hot. It took us a little longer to pack without Sam, but we got it done.

Mom screamed.

A rattlesnake had coiled by her backpack and sat in the shade. My heart fluttered as the thing rattled. I just wanted to be out of here, away from the snakes and scorpions and the sun, in a nice restaurant with my feet up, having waiters serve me.

We tried to grab the backpack, but the snake moved toward us. We waited for it to leave, but the thing had found its shade and wasn't budging. Even though Mom protested, Bryce said he knew what to do.

He took his walking pole and put it in front of the snake's head as he lifted the backpack away. The rattler struck at the pole, probably giving him a fang ache.

I couldn't help looking back to see if the snake was following us.

Mom held Dylan's hand as we walked toward a plateau. It wasn't difficult hiking, but with my feet feeling like bruised tomatoes, walking to the refrigerator at home would have hurt.

Bryce tapped my back with his walking pole and pointed into a ravine. Down the edge, stuck in a juniper tree, was Dylan's Huggy Bear.

"No way we're getting that," Bryce said.

"Could an animal have done that?"

He nodded. "Big one named Sheila. At least we know she came this way."

"You two keep up," Mom yelled.

I kept looking for Sam, but all I saw were footprints and scratches in the rock where people put their walking poles. The trail led into a canyon full of boulders and caves. A cliff dropped at least 100 feet to our right.

Mom grabbed one of Dylan's hands and held tight. "We're going to have to carry him soon," she said.

"Sam will be back," Bryce said.

I wanted to believe it.

"Remember when Ricky was on our boat, the night we confronted him?" Bryce said. "We accused him of stealing the necklace. All of a sudden he got sick and went to the bathroom. Then we started feeling like we were being followed, both on the lake and when we got here."

"You think Ricky got away from the police?"

"No, but what if Ricky wasn't the only one who knew he wasn't sick? What if Sheila or even her mom and dad were in on this?"

"I have a feeling she and the Lord are not on as good of speaking terms as she lets on," I said.

"Stay on the trail," Mom shouted.

"Huggy Bear," I said, finally putting it together. "Dylan couldn't find his Huggy Bear the night Ricky was on the boat. It was in the bathroom, remember?"

"Yeah, but—"

"What if Ricky had the necklace with him on our boat? What if he stashed it in . . ."

I stopped in front of a crevice when I saw someone sitting behind a rock. Short red hair. The woman pulled a water bottle out of her backpack and dumped it over her head.

Our water bottle.

CHAPTER 75

☺ *Bryce* ☺

I couldn't believe it. Sheila just kept pouring water over her head. We waved at Mom when she looked back, and she turned and joined us. When I cleared my throat, Sheila looked up.

"You took our water," I said. "And Dylan's Huggy Bear."

She stood and stared at us, but instead of the sweet, engaged girl who'd been jilted by her thieving fiancé, she looked hard.

"Did you see my husband?" Mom said, out of breath.

Sheila shrugged.

"You took our water, Sheila. Do you have any idea what happens to people out here without water?"

"Where's my Huggy?" Dylan said.

"I didn't take your backpack, little guy," she said.

Ashley stepped forward. "Mom, I don't think she's who she says she is. She knew all along Ricky wasn't sick. They planned the whole thing together."

Sheila smirked and shook her head. "We would have been fine if you hadn't come along. Ricky wanted to leave as soon as the job was done, but we figured you guys would notice and tell somebody, so we stuck around."

Why was Sheila telling us all this? All we had to do was get to civilization and describe her and her cohorts.

Mom pushed Dylan in front of me and moved toward Sheila. "Give us the rest of our water."

Sheila cocked her head. "I'm not giving you anything."

Mom's voice was shaky now. "Just give it to us and we'll be on our way."

Sheila reached inside her backpack, but she didn't pull out water.

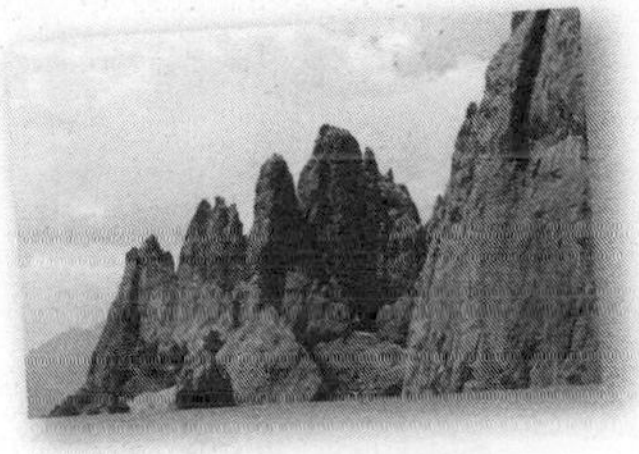

CHAPTER 76

❀ Ashley ❀

I stiffened as Sheila pointed a gun at us.

She turned us around, picking up her backpack and moving us back farther. "Give me more water," she said.

Bryce tensed, as if thinking of jumping her. She must have sensed it because she glared at him. "Don't get any ideas."

Mom gathered Dylan to her like a hen. "We'll die out here."

"Don't blame me. You had to go and stick your noses where they didn't belong. Now hand over the water."

"Why are you being so mean?" Dylan said.

Sheila smiled, but she kept the gun aimed at Mom.

"You take our water and you're basically shooting us," Bryce said.

"Shut up and let me see how much you have," she said.

Between the three of us we were carrying about two liters. Sheila had Bryce and me toss our bottles over, and she poured them into hers.

"Don't move for half an hour," she said. "I'll be watching. Good luck."

CHAPTER 77

☺ *Bryce* ☺

When Sheila had been gone a few minutes, I saw her back-pack disappear around a boulder at the top of the trail.

Mom looked miserable. "I don't know why I brought us down here."

"Let's get going," I said.

"We should stay here," Mom said. "Sam will find us."

I stared at her. "How much water did he have with him?"

"Not much."

"What if he doesn't make it to more?" Ashley said.

"I'm hot," Dylan said.

I took out the GPS and studied where we were. "Sam has only a map. And there's a chance he might crash in the heat. We have to come up with a plan."

"Bryce, we're not going to separate," Mom said.

"We already have, and most of our water is gone. If we don't do something . . ."

"What are you suggesting?" Ashley said.

I showed her the GPS. "The ranger said if we get in trouble the best thing to do is head for the river."

"Bryce, I'm not letting you—"

"It's downhill. It won't be that hard."

"I'm not letting you go alone," Ashley said.

"This is ridiculous," Mom said. "Sam will be back, and then we'll have to come looking for you two."

Suddenly Mom coughed and turned away. She coughed again, and up came her breakfast. She sat on a rock and fanned herself. A raven screeched. The shade was receding as the sun moved higher.

I knelt. "Mom. You know I'm right. We stay here and all of us are going to get sick. Then we'll drink our water, and then what?"

"Someone will find us," she said weakly.

Ashley walked out to the trail. "Sam!" she yelled.

Her voice ricocheted like a bullet off the rocks and through the canyon. This place had filled me with awe. Now it felt like a death trap.

We put all the water in one container. Then I carefully poured out what I would need for the trek to the river and stashed the bottle and purifier pump in my backpack. Ashley tipped the main jug to her bottle, but Dylan moved just as she got it close and knocked it. I watched in horror as a good cupful splashed on the ground.

Ashley yelled at Dylan. I yelled at Ashley. Mom cradled Dylan and rocked him. It was one of the worst minutes of my life.

Dylan's face wrinkled into a prune and he glared at Ashley. "You hurt my feelings," he said, crying.

"Stop crying," I said. "You're wasting water."

That made Dylan giggle.

Ashley knelt near him and took his hand. "I'm sorry."

Mom said, "Why don't you see if you can find Sam before you head for the river."

Ashley and I took off, following Sheila's path up a steep incline. It led to a rock wall that towered over us. Scrub brush and cactus and rocks lay here and there. Since I had the GPS and could see the winding trail in the distance, I suggested we cut across to save time.

We'd gone only a few yards when Ashley pulled up. "Look at your shoes."

All over my laces were spiny burrs, almost too small to see. I pulled a few of them off, and they stuck my fingers. We headed back to the trail.

We reached the top of the trail about 20 minutes later. In the distance Sheila, a tiny dot, moved past another canyon. Ashley and I yelled our lungs out for Sam.

Something glinted by the trail, and I left Ashley to investigate. It was an empty water bottle—the one Sam had taken.

CHAPTER 78

✖ Ashley ✖

Dylan was asleep in Mom's lap when we got back. Mom perked up when Bryce and I came around the rocks, but her face fell when we told her we hadn't seen Sam. We hugged and said tearful good-byes.

I followed Bryce with blurry eyes, matching him step for step. It was the hottest part of the day, the time when you're supposed to find shade and rest, but we had to do this.

We came to a crossing with a wooden sign. A thermometer read 117 degrees.

"It's cooling," Bryce said. He looked at the GPS, clicked it a couple of times, and showed me the screen. "This is the quickest route to the river. All we have to do is follow this."

"What if there are no rafts floating by?"

"At least we get water. And we pray."

I looked at the map as we walked farther. "Bryce, we're heading right for Hermit Creek. Right here—Breezy Point is a campground. They'd have water."

Bryce took the map, punched in the coordinates, and nodded. "It's a risk, but you may be right."

All I could think about was my next step and how long it would be before I could take a drink of water. Bryce kept time on his watch, and every 10 minutes we took a sip.

Would my yelling at Dylan be the last thing he remembered about me?

Bryce dug his walking pole in the ground and leaned heavily on it. He wobbled and threw up.

"That seems to be catching," I said.

His eyes were red and puffy. "I didn't tell you," he said. "I found Sam's water bottle by the side of the trail."

That made *me* want to throw up. I hadn't allowed the thought of Sam not making it to enter my mind.

"Let's keep moving," I said.

CHAPTER 79

◑ *Bryce* ◑

Tossing your cookies in front of your sister is embarrassing, but out here it almost didn't matter.

"Can't wait to get to the hotel and take a long shower," I said.

"I'm going to order 50 glasses of ice water," Ashley said.

We talked about people we were looking forward to seeing at school. We agreed it would be nice to bring Boo Heckler to the Grand Canyon and leave him for a while. He's the meanest kid in our school.

"Time for another sip," I said.

"That's about all I have left."

We came upon some shade, which felt like a gift from heaven.

Ashley held up a hand. "Hear that?"

Something rippled, trickled, and dribbled.

We raced each other to the water, a stream that lay behind the trees. Though the water was only a few inches deep and about four feet wide, we fell into it. No rich person in a spa could have felt as good as I did.

I got out the water filter, and we took turns pumping it into our containers. Stuffing the full bottles in our backpacks and putting them on made us feel like mules instead of just smelling like them, but what a relief, knowing we had plenty of the lifesaving liquid.

"Next stop, Mom and Dylan," I said.

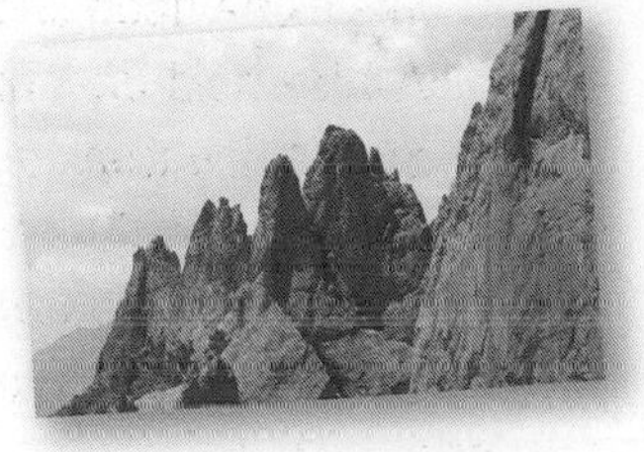

CHAPTER 80

❀ Ashley ❀

Going back up the trail was twice as hard with all the water, but Bryce and I moved like racehorses instead of pack mules. I couldn't wait to see Mom's face and give her and Dylan a drink. I was going to apologize again for yelling and pour water all over him.

Once we were afraid we were lost, and Bryce and I studied the GPS and the compass. Finally I pointed to a triangle of rocks placed so you could see where the trail went. "The cairn," I said.

Bryce shook his head and followed me. We were back on track and finally seeing things we'd missed earlier.

We hollered for Mom and Dylan when we saw the rocks in the

distance. We thought they'd come out to greet us, but maybe they'd fallen asleep.

We made it to the rocks, but Mom and Dylan weren't there. Our stuff sat on the ground alongside an empty water bottle.

"They could have gone that way," Bryce said, pointing off the path. The plateau led to a steep hill that angled down, then dropped into the canyon.

"You don't think . . . ?"

"I see footprints," Bryce said, "but I don't know."

"Please, God . . . ," I whispered.

We took off our packs and put them with Mom's things. Then we heard footsteps. I rushed out.

It was Sheila, half dead, lips parched, wobbling, and out of water.

CHAPTER 81

☾ *Bryce* ☾

Sheila pulled the gun out of her shorts and staggered to a stop. "Water," she said, slurring. She nearly fell but managed to steady herself against a rock.

"Have you seen my mom and Dylan?" Ashley said.

"Water!" she said, waving the gun.

I picked up my pack, filled with water bottles, and got a good grip. It must have weighed a good 30 pounds, and when I threw it at Sheila she raised her arms and the pack hit her right in the face. The gun clattered away, and she crumpled against the rock, swearing.

I grabbed the gun, turned on the safety, and emptied the bullets into my hand. I went out to the edge of the chasm and hesitated. I figured the park rangers would understand. I tossed the bullets over the edge.

Ashley unzipped her backpack and gave Sheila a drink. Talk about loving your enemies and doing good to those who despitefully use you.

Sheila snarled and said she wanted her gun back.

"Where's our mom and brother?" I said.

She shook her head.

I seized her backpack and unzipped it. She tried to reach for it but was so weak she fell at my feet.

Inside I found an empty soda bottle, a bigger empty water bottle (ours), and a sweatshirt that weighed more than a sweatshirt should weigh. I unrolled it and pulled out a gleaming gold necklace.

"Give me that!" Sheila yelled.

"Let's find Mom and Dylan, Ash," I said, draping the necklace around my neck.

CHAPTER 82

❀ Ashley ❀

Mom had to have been in bad shape to move from her resting spot. Bryce and I left Sheila in the shade with enough water to keep her alive.

We hopped from one boulder to another as the trail wound around a rock wall. A huge rock spire that reached to the heavens like some monument to lost civilizations stood to our left.

"Mom?" we shouted. "Dylan?"

Our voices echoed through the desolate area. Then came a weak, "Bryce. Ashley. Up here."

We raced forward, the gold necklace clanging against the GPS

Bryce also had around his neck. The sun was nearing the top of the canyon. In a few more minutes we'd find shade.

Mom and Dylan huddled in a patch of shade the size of a car door. Mom smiled and reached to gather us in.

"You found my necklace!" Dylan said.

"Your necklace?" Bryce said.

"Yeah, it was in my Huggy Bear. It's mine."

We gave them both water, but they drank too fast and threw up. The sun moved over the rocks, and the temperature slowly started to drop.

"Why did you move?" Bryce said.

"Dylan thought he heard Sam." Her chin quivered. "I thought we were going to die. We found this shade, then heard footsteps. I saw Sheila, and we stayed quiet until she passed."

Bryce grabbed a water bottle. "Stay here," he said.

CHAPTER 83

◔ *Bryce* ◔

Dylan had thought he heard Sam, and the little guy's ears were better than Mom's. If Sam had gotten in trouble, he'd do anything to get back to us.

I called his name as I headed up the Hermit Trail. The path got rockier and rougher, and I used my walking pole as I maneuvered over several large stones in a narrow path. I was through it when I heard something—a whisper. I moved to the other side of the rock and saw a boot sticking out.

Sam's boot.

He had crawled into the shade and looked like he had passed out. His water bottle was drained.

"Sam!" I said, opening my backpack and pouring water on his face.

"Hit a wall," he managed. "Tried to make it to water, then turned around when I saw that girl."

"We took care of her," I said. "Everybody's all right."

It was weird seeing someone like Sam lying helpless. That's what the sun can do. I helped him sit up.

Within a few minutes he was drinking water and talking clearly. I took the necklace off and put it around his neck.

I left him there and went for the others. While they headed toward him, I went back for Mom's backpack and to find Sheila. But when I got there, she was gone.

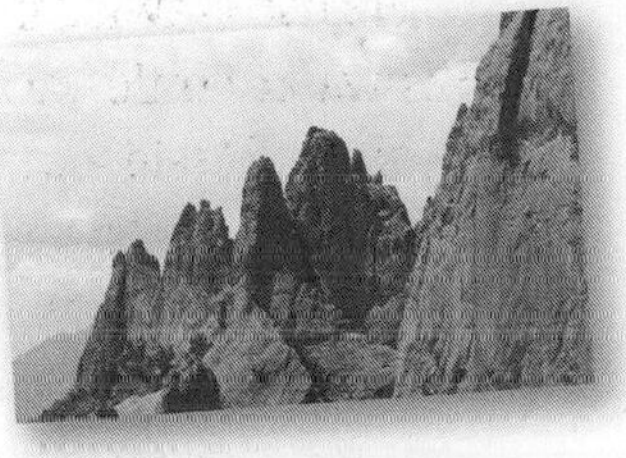

CHAPTER 84

❀ Ashley ❀

Bryce and I switched off carrying Dylan. Mom and Sam basically wrapped themselves around each other and followed us.

When we finally came to Santa Maria Spring it was like reaching the gates of heaven. We plopped down beside two guys from Chicago who were heading into the canyon for a week. It turned out that one of them was a pastor, and the other was his brother-in-law. As soon as they heard what we'd been through, they volunteered to carry Dylan to the top of the trail.

Mom nearly cried when the pastor left his stuff and carried her backpack and the other guy put Dylan on his shoulders. When we reached Hermit's Rest and the parking lot, we were so relieved we just stood there and cried.

Sam offered to pay the guys, but they refused. Mom got their addresses and promised to send books to their wives. That they accepted. They also said they'd keep an eye out for Sheila.

We caught the next bus to our hotel. We took showers while Sam called the police. By nine we were in the restaurant. Sam and Mom had steak and lobster and let us order whatever we wanted. Mom said it was a celebration of surviving not just the hike but Sheila too.

The police showed up and took the "evidence" from Sam. He hadn't said how much the necklace was worth, and when the officer saw it his eyes almost popped out of his head.

I opened my journal and tried to pick up where I'd left off on the trail. I got only a few sentences down before my head hit the pillow. The last thing I remember is Dylan's heavy breathing, Sam turning the TV off, and Mom whispering, "Thank you, God."

CHAPTER 05

☻ *Bryce* ☻

We'd been home two days when we got a call from an agent in New York, calling on Griffin's behalf to thank us for finding the necklace. The man offered a reward and wanted to fly us to the US Open, but Ashley and I didn't feel like traveling yet.

"We'll find something to thank you for your trouble," the man said.

Ashley found a news story from Arizona that said a young woman had been evacuated from the Colorado River after being bitten by a rattlesnake. Except that when medical personnel tried to treat her, she refused and staff at the local clinic got suspicious. They called the police, but the woman had slipped away.

They found "Sheila Lester, aka Shirley Moncrief, aka Sally Ward" in a hotel room with another man and woman and a cache of items stolen from area tourists. Sheila was severely sunburned, dehydrated, and telling a story about two kids robbing her at gunpoint in the Grand Canyon. She said she had come to, thinking she'd been bitten by a snake, but it must have been a bee or a cactus.

"Those cacti are known to jump up and bite you if you're not careful," Sam said.

Mom made a scrapbook of all the pictures we took in the canyon. I had my favorites, but Leigh grabbed the best one of the time-capsule box we dug up. She studied it a long time, then took it to her room.

Dylan got another Huggy Bear. Mom even bought him a special necklace that looked like the one he thought was his. Of course it didn't cost even 10 dollars.

Mom suffered a lot of damage to her feet and toes, and the doctor said it was because of not having her shoes laced tight and because she apparently didn't walk heel first on the hike. Sam didn't say, "I told you so," and it was probably the nicest—and smartest—thing he'd ever done.

A couple of weeks later we gathered in the living room to watch the first round of the US Open. Onto the court walked Griffin wearing more jewelry than Zales.

"My necklace!" Dylan yelled.

The camera focused on Skylar in the stands. "And there's his new wife," the announcer said. "They were married a couple of days ago, and you can bet Mrs. McElroy will be rooting for her new husband to win it all."

Griffin lost in the quarterfinals, and he offered his usual explanation, saying he'd had a bad day rather than admitting his opponent had actually played better and beaten him.

A few days later Ashley and I got a big package from FedEx. Inside were two rackets signed by Griffin and two small tennis necklaces.

Mom took one last picture for the vacation book with us holding the rackets and wearing the necklaces. Underneath she wrote, *The two champs of Lake Powell and the Grand Canyon.*

Mom's book about pioneers and the Grand Canyon sold well and received good reviews. Readers especially liked the part about two young children saving their mother from death.

Authors' Note

This book is dedicated to a number of people who vacationed either in the Grand Canyon or on Lake Powell. We used many of their experiences and the locations of some of their mishaps. We've taken liberties with certain landmarks and locations, so don't try to duplicate the travels of Bryce and Ashley.

If, however, you're inspired to hike the Grand Canyon because of their exciting adventure, remember that many have died because they simply weren't prepared for the conditions. Many excellent books and online resources can help make your trip safe and enjoyable.

About the Authors

Jerry B. Jenkins (jerryjenkins.com) is the writer of the Left Behind series. He owns the Jerry B. Jenkins Christian Writers Guild, an organization dedicated to mentoring aspiring authors. Former vice president for publishing for the Moody Bible Institute of Chicago, he also served many years as editor of *Moody* magazine and is now Moody's writer-at-large.

His writing has appeared in publications as varied as *Reader's Digest, Parade, Guideposts,* in-flight magazines, and dozens of other periodicals. Jenkins's biographies include books with Billy Graham, Hank Aaron, Bill Gaither, Luis Palau, Walter Payton, Orel Hershiser, and Nolan Ryan, among many others. His books appear regularly on the *New York Times, USA Today, Wall Street Journal,* and *Publishers Weekly* best-seller lists.

Jerry is also the writer of the nationally syndicated sports story comic strip *Gil Thorp,* distributed to newspapers across the United States by Tribune Media Services.

Jerry and his wife, Dianna, live in Colorado and have three grown sons and three grandchildren.

Chris Fabry is a writer and broadcaster who lives in Colorado. He has written more than 40 books, including collaboration on the Left Behind: The Kids series.

You may have heard his voice on Focus on the Family, Moody Broadcasting, or Love Worth Finding. He has also written for Adventures in Odyssey and Radio Theatre.

Chris is a graduate of the W. Page Pitt School of Journalism at Marshall University in Huntington, West Virginia. He and his wife, Andrea, have been married 22 years and have nine children, two birds, two dogs, and one cat.

RED ROCK MYSTERIES

BRYCE AND ASHLEY TIMBERLINE are normal 13-year-old twins, except for one thing—they discover action-packed mystery wherever they go. Wanting to get to the bottom of any mystery, these twins find themselves on a nonstop search for truth.

The Wormling

From the minds of Jerry B. Jenkins and Chris Fabry comes a thrilling new action-packed fantasy that pits ultimate evil against ultimate good.

Book I
The Book of the King

Book II
The Sword of the Wormling

Book III
The Changeling

Book IV
The Minions of Time

Book V
The Author's Blood

All 5 books available now!